"We have a wedding this weekend and today the caterer almost quit."

"But you brought them back on board," Max said.

Sierra nodded. "Yes, I did. I didn't want this job. I'm not a romantic. I am the last person who should be planning other people's happy-ever-afters."

"Why's that?" he asked.

She shrugged, unsure of how to answer him. She'd never been coveted, guarded, cherished.

"Until I came to Mercy Ranch, I didn't know any happy marriages or couples who cherished each other. You have this lovely, kind and supportive family. You have the dream."

"I do," he admitted, looking somewhat shy. "I almost threw it all away. But about you. Now that you have the job and since you've been here, in Hope?" he asked. "Now do you believe in happy-ever-after?"

"Sometimes."

She had never really thought about it, but deep down inside, she wanted to believe it existed.

Brenda Minton lives in the Ozarks with her husband, children, cats, dogs and strays. She is a pastor's wife, Sunday-school teacher, coffee addict and sleep deprived. Not in that order. Her dream to be an author for Harlequin started somewhere in the pages of a romance novel about a young American woman stranded in a Spanish castle. Her dreams came true, and twenty-plus books later, she is an author hoping to inspire young girls to dream.

Books by Brenda Minton

Love Inspired

Mercy Ranch

Reunited with the Rancher
The Rancher's Christmas Match
Her Oklahoma Rancher
The Rancher's Holiday Hope

Bluebonnet Springs

Second Chance Rancher
The Rancher's Christmas Bride
The Rancher's Secret Child

Martin's Crossing

A Rancher for Christmas
The Rancher Takes a Bride
The Rancher's Second Chance
The Rancher's First Love
Her Rancher Bodyguard
Her Guardian Rancher

Visit the Author Profile page at Harlequin.com for more titles.

The Rancher's Holiday Hope

Brenda Minton

Recycling programs
for this product may
not exist in your area.

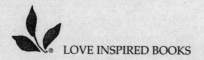 LOVE INSPIRED BOOKS

ISBN-13: 978-1-335-47957-0

The Rancher's Holiday Hope

www.Harlequin.com

Printed in U.S.A.

It is of the Lord's mercies that we are not
consumed, because his compassions fail not.
They are new every morning:
great is thy faithfulness.
—*Lamentations* 3:22–23

This book is dedicated to those looking
for love, for forgiveness, for healing.
I pray you find peace, forgiveness,
healing and a love that is enduring.

Chapter One

Standing in the middle of the Mercy Ranch Wedding Chapel, Sierra Lawson felt almost at peace, as if God was present and this was a real chapel, not just a wedding venue. The building looked more like a stable than a church, but there was something about the sun filtering through the stained-glass windows that touched her soul.

She'd never expected this to be her healing place. One year ago she would have denied she needed healing of any kind. Now she felt as if she was one step closer to being the person she'd always wanted to be. A person who didn't allow others to control her happiness.

She moved to the row of windows that faced east and thought about those horrible days that had changed her life forever just four years earlier. For two weeks she had waited each morning for the sliver of sunlight to appear in her cell. Each of those precious sunrises had marked one more day, one more chance to be rescued, one more day of hoping God heard her feeble prayers as she huddled in an enemy prison in Afghanistan.

Nothing had been the same for her since. It would never be the same. During her weeks of captivity she'd known fear, pain and helplessness. But she'd also known an unexplainable calm and a hope that didn't make sense.

It was because of that experience that she had found her way to Mercy Ranch, a home for wounded veterans just outside of Hope, Oklahoma. And it was due to the ranch owner, Jack West, that she found herself in the position of wedding planner.

Wedding planner? She still couldn't believe she'd agreed to take this on. This was the absolute worst job for a woman like Sierra. She was responsible for selling the dream of fairy-tale weddings and happily-ever-afters. Neither of which was something she believed in. She'd seen too much, been through too much, to allow herself to get caught up in those dreams.

The stillness of the November morning and her quiet reflection was shattered by the steady thump of rotors beating against the air. Sierra backed away from the window and the all too familiar vibration. She waited for the sound of metal and glass hitting hard-packed earth. She tried to convince herself that it had to be a dream. She wasn't in Afghanistan. The helicopter couldn't be real. She was not in danger.

It was the wind beating against something outside. It was late November in Oklahoma and the wind blew on a daily basis.

Somewhere in the building a door banged shut. Glory, her young assistant, must have arrived early to help with the latest community project. Jack West wanted to bring all of the churches in the area together in a massive Christmas event that would include music, a dinner and gifts for children in the community. It was a big project that made Sierra shudder.

Cautious, she stepped into the entry and looked around. When she saw nothing suspicious, she moved to close the doors but before she could reach them a sound behind her had her spinning to meet whoever had entered the building.

Overhead the helicopter still hovered. She caught sight of it out of the corner of her eye. And standing in front of her, a very real little girl.

The girl couldn't have been more than eight. The dog next to her was older. The shepherd had grayed the way an old man would and the look in his expressive brown eyes said he knew he had to protect the small person at his side.

"Hello. Can I help you?" Sierra asked as her heart thudded in time with the beat of the rotors.

She sounded calm. She took some pride in that. She focused on breathing and what she knew to be reality. The helicopter wasn't an enemy attacking. Her brain was telling her to flee, to grab the child and run. That was the wrong response. But knowing didn't stop the panic, the urge toward fight or flight.

If she did what her brain wanted, everyone would think she had finally lost it.

She somehow managed a smile for the child who continued to stare at her, blond hair a tangled mess around a rosy-cheeked face.

"Do you have a name?" The words came out hoarse, not soft and soothing. Her friend Kylie West often used those words on frightened children but somehow Kylie always seemed to calm.

With the question, the child backed away, proving that Sierra didn't have the touch when it came to children.

She tried again. "I'm not going to hurt you."

The little girl didn't seem convinced, even with a softened tone of voice.

"My name is Sierra. I work here. How did you get here?"

The child looked down at her dog.

"Did he bring you?"

No response. Sierra closed her eyes just briefly. When she opened them, the child had started to inch along the wall. Sierra squatted, putting herself at the little girl's eye level. The helicopter had landed. She could see it in the open lawn. Her heart rate slowly returned to normal, as if catching the rhythm of the slowing rotors.

"I'm not going to hurt you or let anyone else hurt you." Sierra hoped the promise made sense.

The little girl ran to her, wrapping thin arms around her neck as the doors to the chapel opened. A less than clean face snuggled against Sierra's shoulder. The child smelled of the outdoors, as if the wind, soil and dog had invaded every pore. Why did children have to smell so bad?

Another wrong thought. The child needed protection. From the man walking through the door? He was tall, dark and not smiling. Handsome. Mind-bogglingly handsome. He had lean features with dark eyes that set her nerves on edge. Definitely not her type. It was more comfortable to think of him as the angry stranger. And his anger seemed to be directed at the child. The dog at her side growled.

The man stopped, removed his cowboy hat and proceeded forward with a calm demeanor. Calm on the surface but with power radiating beneath that outward facade. Sierra didn't know who he was but she found herself wishing she'd taken the child and hidden from him.

"Linnie, we've been looking for you." He spoke with a quiet voice, one that he probably thought would calm the child.

The child—Linnie—shook her head and didn't look up. Her face stayed buried in Sierra's shoulder.

"Your mom is worried sick," he continued.

Sierra felt little arms tighten around her neck. She tried to extricate herself from the vise grip but Linnie wouldn't let go.

"Linnie, your mom called for us to help find you."

The child's body went limp and she curled against Sierra. "Mommy," she whimpered.

"Maybe I should ask who *you* are?" Sierra said, lifting the child as she stood up. The dog stayed close, his growl keeping the cowboy with the chocolate-brown curls at a distance.

Sierra fought the urge to fall apart. He was too dark, too imposing, and the helicopter had already started unraveling her emotions. She backed toward her office door.

"You're not going to take that child," he warned. His voice was low, authoritative. He wasn't used to being questioned.

"I'm not taking her. I'm keeping her safe."

"From me?" He laughed. "I'm the person searching for her. We spotted her from the air as she headed this way."

"And I'm her new best friend."

"The police are helping us search." His voice remained quiet, soothing, but she heard the edge of impatience. "I'll call the sheriff and he can explain the situation to you."

"You go ahead. I'm not giving her up until I know she's safe."

"Suit yourself. But if you have a blanket, she's probably cold. And hungry. She wandered off yesterday evening. She'd been playing in her backyard with the dog and must have decided to go exploring. Her name is Linnie."

Sierra glanced down at the child in her arms. "I'll take her to my office."

"Do I look like someone who would kidnap a child? Whisk her away in my helicopter?" the stranger said.

"It's a crazy world," Sierra responded as she moved away with Linnie clinging to her neck.

"Yes, it is." He followed her into her office.

Sierra held the little girl in one arm while she poured hot water into a cup that she'd prepared with her favorite herbal tea. The aroma filled the air, fruity and light.

"This will warm you up. And I have donuts." She handed one to the girl clinging to her for all she was worth. A dirty hand released its hold on Sierra's neck and grabbed the powdered-sugar-covered donut.

Sierra heard the crunch of tires on gravel and moved to the window as Linnie made short work of her breakfast. A county deputy had pulled up out front. She ignored the man still standing at the door to her office, watching her.

The officer got out of his car, spoke into his radio and then headed for the front door of the building. Sierra made quick eye contact with the cowboy who'd invaded her space. He gave her an "I told you so" look before stepping into the entryway to greet the deputy.

"We've found her. If you could convince the woman inside to hand her over to us," he said as he led the officer through the door of her office.

"Sierra, looks like you found our missing child." Deputy Coleson smiled first at Sierra and then at the child in her arms. "Linnie, your momma is worried sick."

Silent tears began to slide down Linnie's cheeks.

"Do you want me to take you to her?" Deputy Coleson offered. "She's waiting at the police station in Hope."

Linnie nodded but she gave a quick look at Sierra, as if asking permission.

"You go with him and he'll take you to your mommy." The child sniffled and held her hand out. Sierra gave her two more donuts and then escorted her to the officer's side.

"I'm sorry, Jeff, I just didn't know what to do." Sierra didn't know how to explain. "Better cautious now than regretful later."

"You're fine, Sierra. I doubt there's a woman alive who would turn her over without asking questions first. Linnie's mom will be thankful that you found her and kept her safe."

"Who is her mom?" Sierra asked as they headed for the front doors of the chapel.

"Patsy Jay. She lives at the Cardinal Roost mobile home park, just down the road. Unfortunately the place is in the middle of a field with no fences and just a short distance from a heavily wooded area. Her mom was outside with Linnie but she stepped inside to turn off the stove. Didn't take Linnie but a few minutes to disappear into the woods."

Sierra nodded. "Thank you. I'd like to check on her later, to make sure she's okay."

"I'm sure she'd like that." Jeff carried the child to his car.

The other man had left, also. She watched as his long-legged stride ate up the ground. He walked with confidence. He owned his world. He didn't suffer from fear as he stepped up into the helicopter.

Before she could turn away, his gaze caught and held hers. She shivered and backed away from the door. She didn't want to be standing there when the helicopter lifted from the ground. She didn't want to hear the rotors beating the air.

She retreated to her office to wait out the fear and the memories.

* * *

"Ready, boss?" Hank, Max's pilot of three years, asked as Max climbed aboard the Airbus.

Max shook his head as he reached for the headset. He sat there for a full minute contemplating the stable that he knew to be a wedding venue. He couldn't walk away. As much as she had irritated him with her unwillingness to hand over the child, he couldn't leave.

He'd known when he returned to Hope, Oklahoma, that there would be people questioning his motives each and every time he tried to do something for the people and the town he cared about. But this woman at the wedding venue had given him a whole different vibe. She feared him for a completely different reason and, if he had to guess, he would say he looked too much like his Assyrian grandparents.

He'd seen the look before. The one of suspicion. But there had been more in her expression. Terror, carefully held in check, contained.

"I'll be right back," he said as he climbed down from the helicopter.

"Need me?" Hank asked.

"No, I've got this." He ducked slightly as he hurried away from the helicopter.

When he reached the building he hesitated, unsure if he had a right to go inside. He could call Isaac West and let him handle this. He could walk away and pretend he hadn't noticed anything off. He could avoid getting involved because that only led to problems. When a man cared too much, women tended to think long term and not a helping hand.

He stepped through the door into the large entry with its vaulted ceilings. No noises greeted him. The woman—Sierra—had disappeared.

He glanced in her office. Empty.

Next he tried the hallway off the main entry. He heard a noise from a room on the end. As he approached he saw that it was a kitchen. He entered the brightly lit room. It appeared empty. He turned and started to leave. Then he saw her. She was sitting next to a worktable, knees drawn to her chest. There was a stark look of terror in her eyes. Her hands covered her ears and she stared as if not seeing him.

He approached cautiously. When he reached her, he crouched to the floor and waited to see if she would notice him. Eventually her head turned slowly, her gaze locking with his.

"Go," she said.

"I'm afraid I can't." The last thing he wanted was to get involved here. But he knew this feral look. It's what happened to a person when they'd seen too much, been exposed to too much. But he also knew she saw an enemy as she perused his features, his dark hair. Maybe an hour from now that look wouldn't be there. But, at this moment, her mind was telling her he was someone to fear.

"Look at me," he said. "You know where you're at."

Her fists curled as if she meant to strike out. But then she curled her arms around her knees, hugging them tight as she shook her head. "Go away. Please."

"I can't. I have to make sure you're okay."

"Why wouldn't I be okay?" she said with a surprising bit of bravado that could have convinced someone else she was just fine.

"I'm not sure, maybe the look in your eyes when I walked through the door a bit ago. Or maybe the fact that you're sitting here practically in fetal position."

"Maybe I was praying."

"Were you?"

She shook her head, one tear finally slipping free. She swiped at it with a finger.

"I never cry," she said quietly, as if to herself.

"Ah, I see. Would you like me to make you a cup of tea?"

"No, I'm fine."

He moved so that his back was against the wall, putting him next to her rather than facing her. He knew from experience that it was best if she didn't feel cornered. Not his own, but the experience of a good friend. His business partner.

Sometimes a person just needed space to pull themselves together.

She breathed deeply and continued to wipe at tears, whether she admitted to crying or not. He got up and made himself at home, finding a cup, tea and sugar. He considered telling her about Roger. Roger had battled PTSD silently, as if it were something to hide, to be ashamed of. Max guessed that to those battling the past, it felt like something to hide.

It shouldn't be hidden. A person with any other disease would seek the comfort and help of family, friends, physicians. He had finally convinced Roger of that.

He made the tea and handed it to her. She studied the cup, studied him. He held his free hand out to her and she shrank back from him. He considered telling her his background. That his grandfather had been an Assyrian Christian minister who'd migrated to America, where they could be free from persecution. Where they could worship without fear of repercussion. Where his wife and daughter would be safe. His daughter, Max's mother, Doreena.

Max's father was a mixed bag of European heritage,

like most Americans. He could trace his father's ancestry to the early colonists.

But he didn't owe this woman explanations. She didn't owe him any, either.

He was just as American as she was. His grandfather had given them the American dream. He didn't ever take that for granted.

He continued to hold his hand out to her, not even considering why he cared. She wasn't his problem.

But he knew that if he did leave, the helicopter would start back up and he had little doubt that the sound would push her over the edge.

She took his hand. Her fingers wrapped around his, firm and strong. He pulled her to her feet and still he held her hand. He found it strangely frail as he clasped it tight, holding on to her as she surveyed her surroundings. She didn't let go.

"You're okay," he assured her.

"Am I?" she said softly, taking the tea from him. "Even with all evidence to the contrary?"

"We all have bad moments."

She sipped the tea and walked away from him. "Really? Has anyone ever found you cowering in a corner?"

"Once," he admitted.

She took a seat at the island that ran the length of the kitchen.

"Really?"

He sat next to her, saw her stiffen at his nearness. "Yes. Really. Once, when I was about eight. A tornado hit the outskirts of Hope."

"You're from Hope?"

"That's what you're taking from my story? I just opened up to you. I exposed my deep-seated fear of storms."

She laughed, the sound soft. "Right. I'm sorry that you're afraid of storms. Do you still struggle with thunder and lightning?"

"Sometimes," he admitted. "Tornadoes are my real fear. You can't control them."

"You're a control freak, so your fear is born out of the need for control and not the storm itself."

"Yes, I guess that must be it. Or the damage they do."

He wanted to ask her what caused her fear, but he knew that it must be personal. She hid it from prying eyes. She covered her tears with jokes.

"Thank you for coming back…?" She gave him a meaningful look.

"Max St. James," he offered.

She gave him a thoughtful look. "St. James. Melody's brother?"

"Yes." He glanced at his watch. "I have to go now. Will you be okay?"

She lifted her tea but didn't take a drink. "Of course. Embarrassed but okay. And if you could do a girl a solid and not tell everyone that you found me cowering in a corner…"

"Your secret is safe with me."

He left her to her tea and her memories. He knew that he would most definitely see her again. The two of them were on a committee together. She just wasn't aware yet. As he left the wedding chapel, he wasn't sure how to feel about spending more time with her. The last thing he wanted to do was make more connections in Hope.

His plan had been to buy back his family ranch and make a quick exit to Dallas. But it seemed like God had other plans for him. He hoped God understood that the last thing he needed were complications.

Chapter Two

Sierra found a chair and pulled it where she knew the
sounds would be more muffled. In a moment the helicopter would take off.

"Brace yourself," she whispered. She shuddered at the
thought of being dragged into the past by memories that
would feel too much like the real thing.

She knew the mechanics of the flashback. The fear
would trigger a response in the brain. The images would
flash and she would confuse past and present. She would
relive the smells, the sounds, the horrors of the accident,
of being taken captive, of watching from a distance as
her only source of help flew away, unable to locate her.

Coping mechanisms. She needed her coping skills.
She held the cup of warm tea, keeping the aromatic blend
close to her face.

Cup in hand, she stood, knowing she couldn't fight
this fear cowering in a corner. She marched out the front
door of the barn just as the massive helicopter whirred
to life, the rotors spinning and the engine winding up to
lift the monster vehicle off the ground.

She could see the men inside, the pilot with his headset, the passenger who stared out the glass door, making

eye contact with her. From the distance he held her gaze. She remembered the color of his eyes. They were the oddest mixture of moss green, brown and gray. Dark eyes but with a light that reminded her of sunshine filtering through a forest canopy. He had short, curly hair, lean, suntanned features. He knew how to control situations. It came naturally to him. He also knew people. He'd immediately seen the fear in her expression.

She knew people, too. Her job in the army had been human intelligence. The irony had been that she wasn't particularly good with people. She was a loner by nature. And yet she'd been very good at her job.

The man holding her gaze was not the enemy. As the helicopter circled, he waved. She waved back. She wouldn't get lost in memories.

As the helicopter cleared the tree line, she began to breathe. She had survived. Making her way to one of the patio sets on the wide stone-tiled front porch, she sat on the wrought-iron chair, and enjoyed the scent and the sounds of country life. The horses grazing in the field, pulling at the drying winter grass. In the distance a tractor moved a big, round bale of hay.

Peace, that's what she'd found here, in Hope. Peace was what she felt a short time later as she retrieved a cup of tea and returned to the front patio to sit and make notes on future events that would be held at the venue. She had a meeting scheduled for four o'clock. In her current state of mind, she almost hoped they would cancel.

Time slipped away as she worked, sipping on tea that had grown tepid. She glanced up when she heard a truck coming down the gravel road from the main house. It stopped and Isaac West jumped out, shoving his hat down on his head as he did. She turned and headed for the front doors of the building. He followed close behind.

"Why are you here?" she asked as she headed to her office.

He caught up with her. "What? I don't look like the kind of guy who just shows up."

"Not generally."

"I am the kind of guy wo can be here for a friend."

"Go. Away." She took a seat behind her desk and picked up a file. "St. James/Barton Wedding" she'd written across the front. Max's sister.

Melody St. James was twenty-five, had been dating Andrew Barton for five years and had her wedding planned to the last detail. That made Sierra's life strangely complicated. When a young woman had been dreaming of her special day for years, it was difficult to help her match reality to her fantasy wedding.

It dawned on her then why Isaac had appeared at just the right moment to bother her. "He sent you, didn't he?"

"He?"

"Max St. James. That's how you arrived at just the right time. Of all the interfering…"

Isaac cleared his throat. "Did you get off to a bad start with my old friend?"

She ignored the question.

"I don't need to be checked on. I'm very capable of taking care of myself."

Isaac kicked back in the chair opposite her and had the nerve to put his booted feet on the corner of the oak desk that happened to be her pride and joy. It was an antique, passed down through generations. Not generations of her family, but a family.

"Get your feet off my desk," she growled.

He quickly moved his feet to the floor. "Are you okay?" he asked, showing his serious side.

"I'm fine."

He studied her. "It wasn't a bad thing he did, caring enough to call and have someone check on you."

"He doesn't know me. It was intrusive. I'm not sure why he felt he had a responsibility to call in a welfare check on me."

Isaac's expression went from serious to amused and she was thankful. Amused, she could deal with.

"You're so prickly sometimes."

"I'm not." She opened the wedding file. "I'm fine and I have work to do."

"Right."

She looked up, seeing the skeptical expression of a man she considered a friend. "I survived it. There, that's honesty for you. I can admit that it took me by surprise. It's been at least a year since I've had a flashback. But I'm still standing and that's a win."

"That's always a win."

"I'm fine," she repeated.

"I never said you weren't," Isaac said with a casual shrug of his shoulders.

Sierra sat back in her chair. She rubbed her hands down her face and sat silent for a moment, face buried, trying to think of something that would put his mind at ease. "I heard the helicopter, but I held it together. I was nice to a child. I made sure she was safe."

"If you were nice to a child, that's a definite win."

"You know I'm not fond of them. And this one—" She shuddered. "She'd been outside and she had that outdoor kid smell. You know the one."

"Yeah, I know." He leaned back, deceptively relaxed. "You have to let people in, you know. Friends. Family. You can't always shut down and keep people out of your space."

"I know that. But I don't trust easily."

He arched a brow. "Isn't that the truth. I'm still not sure if you trust me."

"I do trust you. I just don't trust you to stay out of my business." She smiled.

They sat there in silence for a few minutes and she knew that there was more. Isaac could be intrusive. He knew when to push. He also knew when to give a person space. He was still here, watching her, waiting.

In the silence, she had too much time to think. Her mind kept replaying the moment when Max St. James walked up to her, dark-skinned, curly hair, piercing gaze. She'd been taken aback by his presence, by him. Unfortunately she hadn't seen the last of him. The file sitting on her desk meant that he would be in her life for the next couple of months as she planned Melody St. James's wedding.

"Will you be at the holiday dinner this Sunday after church?" Isaac finally asked, breaking the silence.

"Holiday dinner?" She had no idea what he was talking about.

"The Hope Community Church holiday dinner. We have it on the last Sunday in November every year. It's open to the community, so we serve food all day, because we never have enough room for one big sit-down dinner."

"And what do you want me to do?" She asked because she knew from his tone that there was more. He wanted her involved. They all did.

"I only want you to join us. We're all still family."

Sierra smiled. The residents of Mercy Ranch were more than family. They'd seen each other through some of the roughest times. They kept one another motivated. In the past couple of years, a few of them had gotten married, including Kylie's marriage to Carson West, Isaac's brother and the oldest son of Jack West. Jack owned and operated Mercy Ranch. It was his way of giving back to soldiers who had fought and been injured.

"You want me to help, don't you?" she asked, knowing his real purpose for bringing up the dinner.

He grinned. "Yeah, I want you to help."

"I'll help," she said. She wasn't excited about it, but it would show them all that she hadn't closed herself off completely.

"Good." He lifted his arm to check the time. "About Max…"

"Another interfering male?" she added.

"No, he isn't. He had a friend, a business associate. Max understands PTSD."

"Right, but I don't need him mucking about in my life."

"Mucking about?"

"Go! I have work to do. Remember, I run this wedding venue for your father. And if you see him, tell him I'm not good at all of this happily-ever-after stuff."

"I think he's hoping it'll rub off on you. I'm starting to think it must be working. A person who says stuff like 'mucking about' has obviously been reading some romance novels."

"I don't believe in romance." She hid her face so he wouldn't see the heat traveling up her cheeks.

"Don't let Max get under your skin. He's not much of a romantic, either. Too busy. I keep telling him women like it when a man shows up. Maybe someday he'll find one he cares enough to show up for."

"I don't need to know about Max St. James." Sierra shot him a look and then picked up the file and walked out of her office. She had a meeting and the last thing she wanted was to have her client's brother on her mind as they met to discuss wedding details.

* * *

Max stood outside the doorway to Sierra Lawson's office, catching the last few sentences of her conversation with Isaac West. He hadn't planned on coming back today, but when he'd gotten home, his sister had informed him she had an appointment at the Stable wedding venue and he had to accompany her because, after all, it was his money she was spending.

He definitely hadn't planned on listening in on a private conversation. But he hadn't walked away quickly enough and had heard his name mentioned. Both were reasons to stay and listen. Now he had to make another decision: make himself known or walk away.

"Max, did you find her?" Melody's question made the decision for him.

"That dirty rat." He heard Sierra gasp, accompanied by Isaac's deep laugh. "Listening in on private conversations."

He stepped into her office, trying hard to be his normal composed self. After all, he was Max St. James. He knew how to keep his expression neutral to make the best deal. He didn't let anything or anyone get under his skin.

So why did he feel like a teenager being called into the principal's office? He pulled on the brim of the cowboy hat he wore and managed to not shuffle his feet.

"I didn't hear much, and most of what I did assured me we won't be best friends."

"Max!" his sister gasped, her eyes widening in surprise. "I apologize for him," she said to Sierra. "He isn't usually this rude."

"I don't need you to defend me, Mel," he told his sister. "I did listen to your conversation. But I didn't mean to. I apologize. And Isaac's portrayal of me is wrong. Mostly wrong."

Sierra glared, her hazel-green eyes dancing with fire. He nearly smiled. Instead he opted for contrite, but, man, it was hard to do.

Sierra glanced from him to Isaac. She didn't say anything and didn't really need to. Her expression said it all. She was angry, cornered and…beautiful.

"I have to get home to my wife." Isaac headed for the door. "Godspeed, my friend."

"Prayers appreciated," Max joked. Because he'd known Isaac most of his life, he knew that Isaac would never let him be "Max St. James, Tech Tycoon." With Isaac, he was just Max, number 32 on the Hope High basketball and baseball teams, a decent partner in team roping and someone most parents warned their kids to steer clear of.

"Men!" Melody snorted as Isaac left. "Now, let's show my brother the venue. He's going to love it so much, he'll want to get married here."

"Oh, are you engaged, Mr. St. James?" Sierra asked, her wide-eyed expression telling him she knew he wasn't.

"No and I have no intentions of getting married anytime soon. Let's have a look at the venue and then we can discuss the plans that have already been made."

Sierra led them through the building that had been built like an overlarge stable. The main area, longer than it was wide and with a cathedral ceiling, was the wedding chapel. What might have been an indoor arena was the reception area. The entire venue was light and airy. Stained glass in the chapel allowed warm, golden light to seep into the large, open room.

Melody talked in great detail about flowers, decorations, food. He tried to focus but it all sounded like she was speaking a foreign language. He'd never expected this from his sister. She'd always been so rational.

He didn't want to interfere but he had doubts about the fiancé who hadn't stepped foot on Oklahoma soil in months. According to Melody, he was busy working in California. Max hoped that was the truth.

"What do you think, Sierra?" Melody had hold of the other woman's arm and he saw Sierra stiffen. But she smiled, as if trying very hard to accommodate his sister's affectionate nature. "Heart-shaped filet mignon or salmon. Isn't that perfect?"

Sierra's face said she thought the idea was anything but perfect.

He swallowed and looked away but not before she gave him a look that begged for assistance. He shrugged but didn't reply, leaving her to come up with an answer for his sister.

"I think that sounds costly," Sierra said. "But of course it's up to you. You're the bride."

"I'm paying for this nonsense," Max inserted. "Why do we need heart-shaped food?"

Melody rolled her eyes. "It isn't about need, it's about want."

"There would be a lot of wasted food," Sierra informed Melody. "They would have to cut the meat to make the heart shape."

"Oh, that is a waste. Okay, nothing heart-shaped except the cakes and cookies for the dessert table. And I'd like to do a traditional dance. My grandmother has been teaching me and she feels very strongly that the dance should be done immediately following the ceremony."

"Traditional dance?" Sierra looked confused.

"Our grandmother is Assyrian," Melody said over her shoulder as she hurried toward the stairs that led to the loft where the bridal party lounge and dressing rooms were located. The groom and his attendants had a separate building. "Our grandparents came to America in the sixties. They're our mother's parents."

Following close behind his sister, Max walked next to Sierra, noticing her thoughtful expression.

"Our grandmother—we call her Nonni—is still very traditional in many ways," Max said.

They had reached the top of the stairs and stopped on the wide landing. Sierra unlocked the double doors and motioned them into the bridal suite, which included a large sitting area and windows offering a brief glimpse of Grand Lake.

"Max, come inside, look around." Melody took hold of his hand and dragged him in.

From the corner of his eye, he caught the expression on Sierra's face. For a moment, she looked sad. He wondered why.

"We should go now," Max told his sister. "I'm sure Ms. Lawson has other clients, other things to do. Not that this hasn't been extremely fun for her."

"I'm sorry, Sierra, I should have realized…" Melody hugged the wedding planner again. His sister didn't notice the other woman freeze up. "I've just been so excited to show Max everything. I knew he wouldn't really appreciate the details, but I knew he'd pretend."

"I'm glad for your sake that he pretended," Sierra said, putting some distance between her and his sister.

"Okay, we'll go, now that my brother is properly impressed. But, Sierra, I would like to extend an invitation to you, to participate in some of our pre-wedding activities."

"Pre-wedding activities?"

Melody walked back down the stairs, staying next to Sierra while Max forged on ahead of them. He knew the look in his sister's eyes, the one that said she had a plan.

"Yes," she went on. "We're sewing a honeymoon blanket. It's a very old Assyrian tradition and my grandmother insisted. We are all taking part. My mother, grandmother, sister, myself, aunts, cousins. My quilt is patchwork, a little of the old country with the new. If you'll join us in the next couple of weeks, just bring maybe a scrap of material from an old shirt of yours. I want to make this blanket about the people in my life."

Sierra opened her mouth as if to object. Max had stopped in the large entry foyer and he watched, waiting for her to come up with an excuse. Not that Melody would accept excuses.

He knew what his sister was up to. She liked the wedding planner, thought she was lonely and in need of someone. And he was that someone. His sister had always been a fixer, even as a child. When he had gone through his destructive teen years, she'd been the one constantly trying to find a way to bring him back to himself. She would plant herself in front of him, demand he stay home and read a book, help her with a school project, anything to try to win him back.

"Melody, it's time to go." He motioned her toward the door.

"Don't get all bossy businessman with me, Maximus St. James."

Sierra laughed a little.

"And this is why I don't like to take her places," he told Sierra. "Time for us to go home, Mel. Nonni is cooking tonight and you know she wants us all there."

Melody gave Sierra another quick hug. He would have to explain to her that she needed to pay more attention to social cues. Sierra Lawson had a bubble and she didn't want people stepping inside it.

He was more than willing to respect her wishes even

if his little sister wasn't. He hadn't come here looking for ties to this community. He'd only come to make amends. Hope, Oklahoma, wasn't his home anymore. In this small town he still felt the past hanging over his head. Everyone knew his stories.

Except Sierra Lawson.

But he doubted she was curious about him. She had her own stories. Stories she didn't seem to want to share with anyone.

That was just fine with him.

Chapter Three

Sierra waited until the church bells rang before she entered the sanctuary and found a seat in the back on Sunday morning. Unfortunately she wasn't the only one sliding in at the last minute. The doors opened and another latecomer entered.

This time Pastor Stevens noticed. He had just made a few announcements but he paused and smiled.

"I know several visitors are with us today. Why don't we take a moment to greet our newcomers, and even those you might not have had a chance to shake hands with."

Sierra groaned.

"Thought you could sneak in unnoticed?" Isaac West asked as he held out a hand. At least he knew she didn't like hugs.

But the huggers were out there, lurking, waiting to wrap warm and welcoming arms around her. She winced at the thought.

"I tried," she admitted.

Before she could say more, she was surrounded. It felt a lot like a mob but she knew it was all about well wishes and not an actual mobbing. She eased away from the push of people, smiling and acknowledging their warm welcome while trying to beat back the claustrophobia that darkened the periphery of her vision. Somehow she managed to speak to an older woman who held her hand, telling her how glad they were to see her.

Someone else reached for her other hand.

She reminded herself that this was good. People were friendly. They were all glad she'd shown up. They didn't know about her past, about growing up in the midst of her parents' destructive relationship or the weeks she'd spent being held captive in Afghanistan.

Taking a deep breath, she managed to smile as she started to back away. She desperately needed space. The urge to be free of the crowd started to claim her in its grip.

"Leave it to me." A solid chest brushed against her back and a deep but concerned voice rumbled near her ear. She didn't turn. She knew who that voice belonged to. She didn't want to rely on him, on anyone.

But now wasn't the time to argue.

"We're going to find our seats now. I think the service is about to start," Max said with an air of authority that had the crowd moving away, reclaiming their seats. His hand, strong and warm, held her arm. The touch grounded her.

She allowed him to take control, moving them to the refuge of a back pew. He released her arm as she took a seat but then he slid in next to her. Of course he did. He'd made it clear that they needed to find a seat before the service started. He'd said, "We're." Didn't he know how small towns worked and that he had given people, even kind and well-meaning people, something to talk about?

"Are you okay?"

She wanted to tell him to mind his own business. That

she could take care of herself. But all of the caustic remarks were buried beneath a layer of gratitude. She rarely allowed anyone to shelter or protect her. She didn't know why it was him, a stranger.

Maybe it was easier to allow a stranger into her life than to lean on friends who had already done so much and knew too much.

"Thank you," she whispered.

He didn't tease or mock. He merely nodded and reached for a hymnal that he handed to her. He took the other one in the back of the pew.

"I'm not always like this," she felt compelled to add.

"I know."

"Do you?" She lowered her voice, aware that one or two heads turned to give her a look. She didn't wait for his answer, instead she joined the singing, not wanting to disrupt the service.

The music seemed to be God's way of drawing her close to Him. It'd always been this way. Even as a child she would make excuses to ride her bike on Sunday morning so she could sit outside the neighborhood church and listen to the congregation sing. She never went in. Her father wouldn't allow that. He hadn't been a believer, so no one else had been allowed to believe.

The music touched the dark, hurting places in ways that sometimes the words of a sermon couldn't. Even now, the music chased away the memories that had started to drag her down. It lightened her soul with words of hope and promise.

The sermon seemed directly related to the last of the hymns, focusing on new beginnings. She closed her eyes at the final words, that new beginnings sometimes required multiple tries. You might have to start again, but as long as you kept moving forward, there was hope.

His mercies are new every morning.

The congregation stood for a closing prayer and then headed toward the fellowship hall.

Again Max walked next to her, his hand on her back, guiding her through the crowd. She didn't need him guarding her. True, he was tall and broad-shouldered, an able bodyguard.

But she knew how to take care of herself. It was safer than relying on someone who might not be there when needed. Or someone who might let you down. She had rescued herself from the nightmare of her parents' divorce. She'd rescued herself from her captors in Afghanistan, managing to overpower a guard as American forces fought to enter the compound.

Yet here she was, allowing Max St. James to lead her through the sea of people, as if he were her Moses, parting the Red Sea for her to get safely to the other side.

"I know you can do this yourself," he murmured very close to her ear. As if he'd heard her thoughts.

"Of course I can."

She kept walking and realized that not once did she feel the dark edges of panic. His hand was on her elbow. He was strong. His presence was real. It was solid. He smelled good, too. Something expensive, with a touch of citrus and mountain air.

People spoke to them as they walked, as if no one noticed anything unusual about the two of them. Or so she thought. As they entered the fellowship hall, she spotted the people who would have questions. Kylie West, once the therapist at Mercy Ranch, and a wounded warrior herself, spotted Sierra and her eyes narrowed. Isaac West, Kylie's brother-in-law, had a more amused expression. And then there was Melody St. James and others that Sierra assumed were Max's family.

The two of them entering this room together was creating a firestorm of speculation. Not something she wanted.

She pulled away from him.

He released her. "You're okay?"

"I am." She meant to say it with a touch of rebuke but it came out softer, as if she were reassuring him. She let it go. "Thank you, for back there. For bailing me out."

"Anytime."

Then he left her and joined his family. An older woman greeted him with a hug, making him bend down so she could kiss his cheek. Sierra guessed her to be Nonni. She was a small woman in a floral dress, with graying dark hair pulled up in a bun. After kissing his cheek, she began to talk, gesturing rapidly with her hands. Melody laughed and gave her grandmother a hug. His parents, whom Sierra had met during initial wedding planning, gave Max hugs. His was a close family.

"Are you going to join us?" Kylie appeared at Sierra's side.

"What?" Sierra pulled her attention away from Max and his family.

Her friend's gaze trailed to the St. James family and returned to study Sierra.

"They're lovely people," Kylie said. "I'm glad they were able to buy back the ranch they sold. This was their home for a long time."

"Yes, it's good they were able to get it back." Sierra clasped her hands together, trying to appear excited. "Let's get this party started, shall we?"

Kylie raised a brow at her enthusiasm. "I'm not buying it, Sierra."

"Oh, come on, you know I love big, festive events."

They both laughed. The laughter shook loose some

of the darker emotions she'd been feeling the past hour and a half. It felt good to have lighter emotions rising to the surface.

"Of course you do." Kylie drew her toward the kitchen. "I thought you could serve desserts. Keep them cut, on plates, ready to be picked up by the guests."

"Sounds easy enough."

"It is easy. You'll get to socialize a little, serve dessert and have fun."

Sierra gave an exaggerated shudder. "Socializing and having fun. Two of my favorite activities."

Kylie showed her all the cakes and pies, the table she would stand at, the plates and cutlery stacked up on the side. And then she looked past Sierra's right shoulder and smiled a little too brightly.

"Here's your helper now!" Kylie exclaimed.

"Helper?"

Warning bells went off in Sierra's head. She looked up from the cake she'd been about to cut, expecting Max St. James. But she was wrong. It was his grandmother.

"Nonni, I'm so glad you can help us." Kylie gave the older woman a hug.

"I'm glad to help. I have so many fond memories of these church dinners." Nonni extended the smile to include Sierra. "And you, the wedding planner, I'm so glad we can finally meet. Melody talks of you constantly."

"I'm not sure why!" Sierra said.

Max's grandmother smiled big. "Because you say what you think."

Sierra felt a rush of warmth slide up her neck. "Oh, there is that."

Nonni patted her arm in a motherly way. "We would like for you to join us, working on the honeymoon quilt. And, also, if we could talk about food. Maybe we can add a few traditional dishes to her reception dinner. I don't want to take over."

"Nonni, don't tell fibs." The deep voice came from behind Sierra. "You always want to take over. They say it's where I got my type A personality."

Nonni's forest green eyes sparkled with joy. "Max, you're going to help us serve dessert?"

"No, I don't think so." He moved to his grandmother's side, smiling at Sierra as he placed a protective arm around his grandmother's shoulders. "I have things to do."

"Watching football isn't a thing to do," Nonni warned. "We're serving dinner today. You can miss the game just once. You and your father. You can help with dessert. Your father can help with cleanup."

"I'm not sure about that," Max countered.

"Oh, I am sure." Nonni smiled brightly and the battle was won.

It happened that quickly. One minute Sierra and Nonni were working the dessert table and Sierra thought it might be fun to get to know this older woman. And the next minute Max became a part of the equation.

Sierra had been backed into a corner. The only upside to the situation? The sweat on Max's forehead as he realized he'd been outmaneuvered by his grandmother.

Nonni had a way of making him feel trapped. He loved her and would do anything for her. Which was the reason he stayed to help serve up cake and pie. He stayed, knowing she had something up her matchmaking sleeve.

Not something. Someone. Specifically, Sierra Lawson. She obviously didn't see why this project had failure written all over it. He wasn't interested. And neither was Sierra.

In his mind, a matchmaker only worked when a person

wanted or needed help finding love. His grandmother, on the other hand, liked a challenge. She seemed willing to try matching the two most unwilling subjects.

Fortunately for him, he had experience dealing with Nonni. Sierra had been taken by surprise. A sneak attack by his grandmother. She'd adjusted quickly, though, and was now listening intently as his grandmother talked about food and recipes.

His grandmother pointed to her *kilecheh.* "These are our Christmas cookies," Nonni told her. "The rolled pastry is filled with dates, the other is filled with nuts, sugar and cardamom. They're very good. Try one."

"I shouldn't." Sierra held a hand up to protest but Nonni stuck a pastry in that protesting hand.

"No, you should. They have no calories at Christmastime." Nonni laughed at her joke. "These are my grandson's favorites."

He reached for one as Nonni watched, waiting for Sierra's response.

"They're very good. Is that a yeast dough?" Sierra asked after finishing the small date-filled pastry.

"It is." His grandmother glowed as she began to tell the younger woman all about her *kilecheh.*

His grandmother loved sharing traditions and loved a willing listener even more.

Sierra asked questions in her serious way. She wasn't a person who gave false compliments, he realized. She seemed very detail-oriented, matter-of-fact in her questioning. He guessed this to be the reason Jack West had given her the job of running the Stable. She also baked. He knew this because Melody had shown him photos of the wedding cakes, going on and on about how amazing and beautiful they were.

He'd half listened because at the time he hadn't met

Sierra. He hadn't known she had hazel eyes, auburn hair and a way of avoiding eye contact when she was uncomfortable. She also had a way of smiling that took a man by surprise.

At that moment she bestowed one of those rare smiles on his grandmother. Nonni beamed and issued another invitation besides helping with the honeymoon quilt. She would love for Sierra to help her bake pastries and cookies for Christmas. It was a large undertaking. Each year his grandmother baked for several days then she would take the baked goods to her old church in Tulsa, to other Assyrians.

His grandmother had a big heart. She loved to nurture. He could see the gleam in her eye. She'd found a likely candidate for all of that nurturing.

Fortunately people started to arrive. His grandmother and Sierra worked side by side, serving cake, cupcakes and pies. As people came up to their table, his grandmother hugged them and doled out compliments and encouragement. Sierra took the role as the quiet one, working to keep the sweet treats flowing.

"Max, we need another cake. Hurry, hurry, slice it up and bring it over." Nonni issued the order without looking.

He turned and nearly tripped over a small child. He recognized her immediately. "Linnie, how are you?"

The little girl with the tangled blond hair now had her curls in a ponytail. She wore a blue dress and tennis shoes. Her eyes flashed with recognition and she gave him a slight smile, but then she started searching for her mother.

"Linnie, there you are." A harried-looking young woman with a baby on her hip, and leading a child a little younger than Linnie, approached.

"You must be Linnie's mom. I'm Max St. James."

Her cheeks turned a bright shade of pink. "Oh, Mr. St. James, I'm so sorry she's bothering you. I've been meaning to thank you for helping us find her."

"I'm not really the one who found her..." He hesitated. "Miss—"

"Oh, I'm sorry. I'm Patsy Jay." She took his hand in a hearty handshake. "I'm so glad to meet you. And I'm so thankful for what you did to help find my daughter."

"Allow me to introduce you to Sierra Lawson. She's the one who actually found Linnie."

He pointed her toward the dessert table and Sierra. Linnie had already spotted her and he watched as Sierra squatted so that she could be eye to eye with the child.

"Hey, Linnie! Imagine seeing you here!" Sierra gave the little girl a warm smile.

Linnie flung her thin arms around Sierra's neck.

"I got in trouble," she told Sierra.

Patsy Jay stepped close to her daughter. "She doesn't usually take to strangers. It's been hard for us since..." Patsy shook her head. "Since the accident. I'm going to nursing school. I'm gone a lot, working and attending classes. My mom watches these three. It's a lot." Her cheeks burned scarlet. "I'm sorry. You didn't need to hear all of that."

Sierra stood and he noticed that Linnie had hold of her hand. "Patsy, you don't have to apologize for doing your best for your family."

Patsy teared up. "Thank you so much. And I wanted to invite you and Mr. St. James to my house for dinner. I live in trailer 12 at the Cardinal Roost. I don't have a lot but I'd like to do something for the two of you."

"Oh, I..." Sierra glanced down at the little hand holding hers.

Patsy bit down on her bottom lip. "I understand if you can't make it."

"Of course we can," Max responded. "When?"

"Thursday at six?" Patsy's hand rested on her daughter's shoulder. "We would like that, wouldn't we, Linnie?"

The little girl nodded.

Sierra handed Linnie a piece of chocolate cake on a small paper plate. "We would love to come to dinner."

The word *we* took Max by surprise. No doubt she didn't mean to make it seem as if they were a couple. They were barely acquaintances. Furthermore, he hadn't been part of a *we* in years. He had a habit of letting women down and he guessed that Sierra had been let down by too many people in her life.

Their gazes connected and he knew that her thoughts had taken the same path as his. If they allowed people to connect them as a couple, things would spiral out of control.

That was the last thing either of them needed, and the one thing Sierra didn't need was to be another person he let down.

Chapter Four

Monday morning Sierra woke up to a clap of thunder that shook the windows. The weather had been warm but a cold front had arrived and the two air masses collided to form one powerful storm system. She prayed it would move through quickly with no real severe weather. With Christmas less than a month away, what they needed was a good cold snap, maybe some snow. But they definitely didn't need damaging winds or tornadoes.

Peeking out the window, she shivered. The sky was one massive dark gray cloud. The storm pounding the side of her apartment required baking.

In the kitchen she flipped on all of the lights, flooding the room in nearly startling brightness. She told the smart speaker to play songs from her panic playlist, smiling at the name she and Kylie had used for the songs that were meant to draw her out of a panic attack. The first song was one she loved to sing along to.

As she sang out loud, she started boiling hot water for her tea and put two slices of bread in the toaster. Next she grabbed a cookbook, the one with all of her favorite cake recipes. She browsed through the pages and finally went to her go-to vanilla cake. A lovely, simple cake made with real vanilla.

She pulled out bowls, beaters, ingredients and lined it all up on the counter. Baking had been her escape for years. As a girl enduring her parents' fights, she would bake. Bake and keep to herself, hiding the shadows of her life so that others couldn't see what was going on inside the lovely brick facade of the Lawson home. Her banker father would leave the house, briefcase in hand, smiling at neighbors. Her mother would slide designer sunglasses on her face to hide the bruises.

Sierra would bake. And eat. Now she baked but she didn't eat the cupcakes, cakes and pies. She gave them away to the other residents of Mercy Ranch, the place she'd called home for the past three years.

She sifted together the dry ingredients, enjoying the process, the smells that changed as she added each one. Vanilla happened to be her favorite.

She prepared the round cake pans and poured the batter in equal amounts. There was another crash of thunder and all the windows rattled from the power of the storm. She nearly dropped the bowl. Her hands shook. She wrapped them in her apron and told herself to be calm, take deep breaths, focus.

From the living room she heard the front door creak on its hinges. She poured water over the tea bag in her cup and walked to the living area. Kylie West waved as she dropped her purse on the sofa.

"I was on my way to breakfast with Maria when I saw lights on and thought there might be coffee."

Sierra headed back to the kitchen to put the cakes in the oven. "You know I don't drink coffee. Come up with a better reason for knocking on my door in the middle of a storm."

"I saw the lights on and thought you might be up, and I wondered, again, why you won't accept a service dog."

"They're messy. They shed. They require too much."

"A Labradoodle doesn't shed, or not much. They give more than they take."

"I'm afraid I would forget to feed it, or water it. That would be terrible. That's also why I don't babysit those cute kids you all seem to like bringing into our lives."

"You're not as unaffected by them as you like to pretend. I've watched you holding Eve's little Tori when they come to visit."

"She's not as stinky as some. And Glory's little bundle of joy, Cara, is okay. When she isn't smelly or crying because she's teething. When did Mercy Ranch become a home for wayward teens and their babies?"

"You're such a phony. You love babies and dogs."

"Make yourself a pot of coffee," Sierra offered. "I'm baking."

She ignored the "Aha! I knew it!" look on Kylie's face. It wasn't easy having a therapist for a best friend. She'd had best friends in her life. Everyone had a best friend in grade school, then high school. But Sierra had never invited friends to her home, not with her parents being how they were. Kylie was the first friend she'd ever been completely honest with. It was refreshing, to have a relationship where she didn't hold back a part of who she was.

It was the reason she didn't date. She didn't want to have a relationship where she couldn't share her true self. She was tired of fighting the past. She'd made huge strides at Mercy Ranch. She had a life here that she loved. She had friends.

Kylie made herself at home, because she'd once lived here. She pulled out the aging coffeepot, got it started, then helped herself to the banana muffins Sierra had made the previous day.

"I thought you were going to breakfast with Maria? Shouldn't you be at your house with your lovely doctor husband and two precious children?" Sierra asked as she poured batter into another cake pan.

"He took them to Holly's Diner for breakfast."

"I see. And…?"

"I wanted to visit with you. I know the last few days have been rough, and then this storm hit."

Sierra placed the two round cake pans in the oven and grabbed her tea to join Kylie at the kitchen island. "I'm fine. Really."

"How'd it go yesterday, serving dessert at church?" A knowing look lit up Kylie's expression. Sierra's friend did not have a poker face.

"Oh, you mean with Nonni?" She wouldn't mention Max St. James.

"Yes, Nonni, of course. She's a sweet lady. The family lived here for years, until they sold the farm and moved back to Tulsa. I'm glad they've returned."

"They seem to be a part of the community already."

Kylie got up to pour herself a cup of coffee. "Yes, I guess they are. And Melody getting married at the ranch seems so right. How are the plans going?"

"She wanted a Christmas wedding. Her fiancé pushed it back to Valentine's Day."

"Why do you seem upset about that?"

Sierra closed her eyes, wishing for once that Kylie had a different job. Why couldn't she be friends with an accountant, a schoolteacher, maybe a nurse? Anything but a therapist?

"Could we have a normal conversation?" Sierra asked.

"Oh, sorry. I'm doing it again, aren't I?"

"You are," Sierra agreed. "So, church was nice yesterday. I enjoyed the music."

"It was. Do you have plans for Christmas?"

Sierra laughed a little. "Same as every year. I'm joining all of you on Christmas Day and hiding the rest of the time." She paused. "Except I seem to have been invited to make cookies with Nonni and I'm also supposed to help sew a honeymoon quilt."

"How fun." Kylie grinned at her over the rim of her coffee cup, trying to hide her amusement.

"Really? Fun?"

"Of course," Kylie agreed. "I have to leave soon, but save me a piece of cake."

"I would, but I'm taking it to Lakeside Manor since it seems some Scrooge is trying to steal Christmas from the residents. I'm going to bake cupcakes for Patsy Jay's children to decorate. I'll make extra for you and the kids."

"Oh, you don't have to. But since you insist..." She flashed another quick smile. "I saw you talking to them yesterday."

Sierra got up to make herself another cup of tea. "Patsy invited Max St. James and me to her house for dinner. She thinks she needs to repay us, although I don't think we really did that much. The little girl wandered onto Mercy Ranch then the police took her home. Has she done this before?"

"I think one other time. I'm glad she had her dog with her."

"Yes." Sierra thought back to her own childhood and the long walks she would take to escape her parents and their fights.

Sierra glanced at the digital clock on the oven. "I need to finish up here and head to the Stable." The Stable, a common name for a very uncommon wedding venue. "I'm going to decorate for Christmas."

"Don't you have another Christmas wedding coming up?"

"Yes, and they want twinkle lights and white poinsettias and trees. White trees! It's a winter wonderland theme."

"Are you going to decorate in here for Christmas?" Kylie asked.

Sierra got up to check on the cakes. The aroma of sugary vanilla goodness filled the kitchen. Aromatherapy. The storm forgotten, she inhaled deeply.

"I am. Glory and Cara are living here, too, and they deserve a tree and gifts." Sierra admired the young mother. She'd started out as a teen mom from a dysfunctional home. For a time Kylie and Carson West were foster parents to Glory's baby. The Wests mentored Glory, helped her to get her life back on track, and she'd regained custody of her daughter.

"Does it bother you that Jack is allowing them to stay? I know Mercy Ranch is designated for military vets, wounded warriors, and Glory is just a teenager who made mistakes."

"She's a wounded warrior of another kind. She battled abuse, addiction, and won. She deserves to be here, too."

Sierra didn't look at her friend. She didn't need a pat on the back or kudos for being kind. She'd spoken the truth.

Knowing Sierra as she did, Kylie merely cleared her throat and moved on. "So about this dinner Thursday, with Max…"

"Stop."

Kylie laughed and didn't look at all ashamed. "You

know he's fabulously wealthy, right? Software, a social media platform, government contracts and so forth."

"You know I don't care about the man's financials, right? He was nice enough to help look for Linnie, and her mother is kind enough to want to thank him."

"He's also handsome."

And he smelled amazing. She cringed at her thought. "I'm not interested."

"Of course not. But someday you will meet someone." Kylie carried her cup to the sink.

"I meet people all the time. I'm not interested in inviting a man into my world, my very fragile hold on sanity. I'm in a good place, Kylie. I don't need a man to make me happy. I don't need to get married and have children. I don't want to repeat—" She cut herself off and just stared at her friend, because the words had rushed out before she could stop them.

"You don't want to repeat your parents' mistakes. I get that. But you should give yourself more credit. You aren't your parents."

"I know."

"If you're looking for the Christmas tree and decorations, they're in the storage room at the back of the building."

"I'll get them out and let Glory do the decorating. She should be home from her aunt's in Tulsa by the first of next week."

"She'll enjoy decorating the apartment." Kylie agreed with the plan. "And you know she's going to hold you to the offer to bake and decorate Christmas cookies for the church Christmas program."

"I know. And I don't mind."

Festive lights, trees, pretty wall hangings. All of the trimmings of Christmas. And now she could add to that baking Assyrian Christmas pastries with an elderly woman affectionately known as Nonni. She wasn't going to lie to herself, though. She wanted to experience the traditions the older woman had passed down to her children and grandchildren.

She knew it would be as if she was standing outside, peeking in, taking a small piece of that family for herself. Her own family had never shared traditions, other than perhaps drinking too much on holidays and ending the day with fighting and uncomfortable silence. Thankfully she'd had decent friends back then, the kind that had shown her a glimpse of real family life.

Sierra walked Kylie to the door. The rain had dwindled to a light mist. The grass glistened with the moisture and, in the distance, the sun tried to peek through the heavy gray clouds.

She remembered the verse, that His mercies were new every morning. Just as quickly as the verse skipped through her mind, hope kindled in her heart. It was a flicker of joy, a strange lightness to her soul. It seemed to come out of nowhere. And yet it was very real. As if spiritually and emotionally she had turned a strange corner and was traveling in a new direction.

Hope. Unexplainable. Unaccountable. Unexpected. It made her wonder, what did God know that she didn't?

Maybe it was the coming holidays? Whatever it was, for the first time in a long while, she found herself hopeful.

Melody caught up with Max as he was heading toward the barn, his boots sloshing in the rain-soaked grass. She was dressed for work, in a pretty sweater over leggings and boots. Somewhere along the way she'd ditched childhood, princess dresses and their mother's high heels and become an adult.

"Shouldn't you be on your way to work? You know, small children expecting their favorite teacher?" he asked.

"Teacher meetings, so I'm going in a little bit late. I was on the phone with Andrew. He's going to try to be here the week after Christmas."

"I see," he said. He pulled gloves out of his pocket and tried to push back the doubts about this fiancé who couldn't even bother to show up and take his sister to dinner. "Dad and I are buying cattle today. Too bad you can't join us."

As a kid she'd loved the sale barn and livestock auctions.

"Oh, I really wish I could but..."

"You've lived in town too long, City Girl."

She laughed. "I haven't. You know I still love the auctions. And I'm not the only one who's lived in the city too long. Look at you, it's almost looking like you still belong here. I like the hat."

It had felt good, getting ready this morning. No suit and tie, just jeans, boots and his favorite cowboy hat. He was used to long hours and long days in an office. Fresh air felt good for a change.

"So what do you really want?" He slowed so that she didn't have to run to keep up with him.

Ahead of them, their dad had the truck hitched to the stock trailer. Aldridge St. James had always been a farmer but he'd traded this for life in town, and a factory job. He'd done what was needed to get Max out of trouble and through college. Then it had been Max's sisters, Melody and Cadence, in college. Cadence had married last year and was living in Texas.

A family ranch traded for the future of his children. Traded for lawyers for his son, who had driven a truck through a school building when he'd drunkenly confused the brake for the gas.

Max had worked hard to get back on track. Now he was giving the life they loved back to his parents. He saw the difference in their expressions. They were able to retire now, knowing they could farm and live in the community they loved so much.

"Well?" he prodded, because Melody still hadn't answered and looked uneasy. "Melody, if you need something, tell me. Is it the wedding?"

"No, of course not. You've done everything for the wedding. I can't even begin to thank you for all your help. Financial and otherwise."

He stopped and waited. "Spit it out."

"Coats for kids. I know you're already invested in helping with the Christmas at the Ranch event. But the weather is getting colder and you'd be amazed at the number of kids who show up to school without a jacket."

"I'll bring it up to the planning committee at the next meeting." And he'd take the curious, sometimes questioning looks that some of the older folks on that committee would give him. He'd been in town for a month and had gotten used to the fact that, to a lot of the people in Hope, he was still the kid who'd crashed a truck through the school. He was still the kid who had driven recklessly, drank too much and hurt the nicest girl in town when he'd left her sitting at home the night of the prom.

"Give me a few days to work on this. You and your friends start putting together names. If I have to, I can call in favors from friends in Dallas."

"Yes!" Her eyes sparkled with excitement. "You're the best, Max."

"I try."

She cocked her head to the side, the way she'd been

doing since childhood. "Max, are you okay? I know it's been hard for you, being here."

"I'm thirty-three, Melody. I've put a lot of years between myself and my mistakes."

"I know. I just think you're still trying to make amends with everyone, and I hope you understand that the past is forgiven."

"I do understand that. Don't worry about me, I'm good. But I want you to know something. If Andrew doesn't show up in town soon, I'm going looking for him and it isn't going to be pretty when I catch him."

"He was here when we first met with Sierra and he will be back soon. He just didn't expect me to take this teaching job in Hope. He likes to have a plan and this wasn't on the list."

"If he's marrying you, he'll have to get used to spur of the moment."

"You're just trying to change the subject," Melody accused her big brother. "And since we're both good at that, isn't Sierra the best? She's on the planning committee for the Christmas event, too, isn't she?"

"I think they're asking for her help, yes."

"I like her," Melody continued. "She is much nicer than she lets on."

"I'm sure she is. And before you continue this, I'm not interested. I'm only here until after Christmas and then I have to get back to Dallas. My company can't run itself, you know."

"You have Roger and you have an assistant. Give yourself a break. And I don't know why you're not interested in her."

His little sister made him dizzy. "First, I'm taking a break while I help Dad get this ranch going again. Second, I'm not interested because I don't have time for a relationship right now. And, third, I'm leaving in a month."

She saluted and looked more determined than ever. "Whatever, Big Brother, whatever. I've got to run. Don't forget the coats. And try being charming once in a while."

He watched Melody walk away and couldn't help but think about Sierra. The last thing she needed was a man who wouldn't be sticking around. She had enough to deal with. He wasn't going to add to the list.

Besides that, Sierra didn't strike him as a woman seeking a relationship. Her expression was guarded and shadows lurked in her eyes, telling more about her past than words ever would. He'd met other wedding planners. They tended to be a perky bunch with great social and organizational skills.

Sierra Lawson didn't fit the mold. Wedding planning seemed to be the last thing she would ever want to do with her life.

She struck him as a loner, the type who had a cat or two, piles of books and a ready excuse for why she preferred to be alone on Christmas. Strike the cats. She wouldn't have cats. Maybe she didn't even have a dog.

She did have friends, though. Isaac, Kylie and the other residents of Mercy Ranch were her friends. She probably kept her circle close and resisted outsiders.

That would be him.

"What did Melody want?" his dad asked, stepping around the back of the stock trailer. He wore a plastic cover over his good hat, to keep the rain off. It was pulled down low, keeping his unshaved face in shadows.

"She wants me to ask the Christmas committee if they can buy coats for children who might be in need." He explained everything his sister had told him and watched as his dad mulled it over.

"I think that's a good idea. You don't mind helping her?"

"I don't mind. If I can help, I should. I've been blessed, Dad. I don't know why, but I do know that God wouldn't want me to sit on what I have and not help those around me."

Aldridge clapped a hand on his shoulder. "I agree. I'm proud of the man you've become."

A short time later he was behind the wheel of the farm truck, dragging the empty stock trailer in the direction of the livestock auction. As he drove, his mind drifted and he found himself thinking about Sierra. Again.

She was a puzzle. She was a woman who protected a child, hid in corners, stared at him as if he were the enemy, then accepted invitations from his grandmother to bake Christmas pastries and work on a honeymoon blanket.

She wasn't his problem to solve.

Chapter Five

Sierra got a call from Jack West on Tuesday. He wanted to have the Christmas planning committee meeting in her office, with her in attendance. Thus far she'd avoided the bimonthly meetings. Now that they were just weeks away from the event, they were bringing her in to help finalize the plans. The group included various community leaders, pastors of the town's churches and Jack's sons, Carson and Isaac West.

Before they arrived, she put on a pot of coffee, set out an assortment of cookies and started dragging extra chairs into her office from the storage room. It was dark, smelled of spiders and dust, and, just in general, it creeped her out.

She grabbed a couple more chairs and scurried from the room just as someone came through the front doors of the building. She jumped and shrieked, not expecting to see anyone standing there.

She hadn't expected to see Max.

"I didn't mean to scare you," he said as he reached for the chairs she still held on to.

"You didn't scare me," she denied. And it was an outright lie. "Okay, a little. I didn't expect you. They're having a Christmas committee meeting and I'm grabbing extra chairs. What are you doing here?"

He grinned. "Surprise!"

"They've put you on the committee?" She wiped her hands down the sides of her jeans, knocking off the dust and hopefully not any spiders. She shook at the thought. Spiders starred in some of her worst memories. She still dreamed of them, crawling around the dark, dank cell she'd been held in during her captivity. She ran her hands up her arms.

"Are you sure you're okay?"

"Mmm-hmm. Yep. Of course."

"I can help you get chairs. I don't mind."

"I only need a few more," she told him as he handed her the two chairs he'd taken from her.

"You take these to your office and I'll get the rest of them."

"Thank you."

He shot her a look. "Well, now, that didn't hurt, did it?"

"I can be polite."

"I wasn't talking about thanking me. I meant allowing me to help."

"Oh, that," she said. "Yes, that *did* hurt."

She started to laugh and it eased the tightness in her chest. She took the chairs to the office, wiped them down and waited for him to return with more. Moments later he did, a cobweb hanging from his cowboy hat.

She wiped down the chairs then reached up to swipe away the web. A spider crawled across his hat.

She jumped back, scrunching her eyes shut. "A spider. On your hat."

He pulled off his hat and headed for the door.

"Kill it!" she yelled.

"It's harmless. I'll brush him off outside."

"It's a spider."

He gave her a look that questioned her sanity. "It's just a spider, Sierra. It isn't going to hurt anyone. It's probably one of the good ones who likes to eat other bugs."

She shook her head, watching as he exited the building, hat in hand.

He returned a few minutes later. "Better?" he asked.

"Absolutely not." She circled him, making sure there were no other spiders hitching a ride.

She was inspecting his shoulders when Isaac West walked through the door with his father. Heat immediately scorched her cheeks.

"He sure is a fine-looking man," Isaac teased. "Any special reason you're inspecting him like a horse at auction?"

"He had a spider on him…" she started to say. Then she saw the teasing glint in Isaac's eyes. "Go away."

Isaac laughed. "Sierra's funny bone was fractured and never healed correctly."

"That wasn't funny." She started to leave but Jack was eyeing her suspiciously. She loved Jack. He'd done so much for all of them. He was the father to everyone on Mercy Ranch. "Hi, Jack."

She would do anything for him. Even be on this committee. Be his wedding planner for however long he thought she needed the job. She believed his goal was to show her happy couples. Over and over and over again.

Jack patted her hand. "Ignore him. He can't help being a doofus."

"I'm not sure how Rebecca puts up with him," Sierra quipped as she led Jack to the office.

"She loves me," Isaac called out.

Sierra knew that to be the truth. She led Jack to her chair behind her desk because it was the most comfortable in the room. Her own father hadn't paid much attention to her, except to yell and occasionally wound her emotionally. He 'd never hit her. That was one thing he'd reserved for her mother.

Jack was the closest thing she'd ever had to a real father. She cherished him for that role in her life.

"Can I get you coffee?" she asked as he settled behind the desk, weak from fighting Parkinson's.

"I'd like a cup," he told her. "And a smile. I asked you to help us because you're just about the most thorough person I know."

She laughed. "I'm a wedding planner, Jack."

His eyes sparkled with humor. "Well, there is that."

The men entered the room, discussing a horse Isaac wanted to buy. Max seemed to be trying to talk him out of it.

"You just want that horse for yourself," Isaac accused.

Max shrugged as he poured himself a cup of coffee and grabbed a cookie. "There might be some truth in that. But that horse came from my dad's first mare. I'd like to build our new herd with him."

"Oh, fine, take advantage of my sentimental side. Buy the horse. But I get the first colt from him."

"Deal." Max held out his hand.

The other committee members started to arrive.

Sierra took a seat off to the side. When Max grabbed a chair and pulled it next to her, she frowned. He merely winked.

Max had met with the planning committee the previous month, when he'd first arrived in town. He knew what to expect. Some of the townspeople were curious about the return of the St. James family. Some were thrilled to have their old neighbors back. More than a few were skeptical of Max and his intentions. He guessed he should expect that.

What he hadn't expected was the father of the girl he'd hurt more than any other. Amy's dad, Davis Stanford, walked into the room and stopped cold. He gave Max a long look then he took his seat next to John Stevens, the new pastor of Hope Community Church.

Max sat listening to the other committee members discuss the gifts that had been collected so far, the donations of money for food, the groups that would sing. The churches that owned buses would help haul families and children who had no other transportation.

Jack cleared his throat. "I have a couple of things to add. First of all, we've all heard about the situation at Lakeside Manor. The new owners of the nursing home seem to be cutting the budget and that affects the residents' Christmas celebrations. I would like to suggest that we transport residents who are able to check themselves out or who have family members capable of checking them out."

"That's a great idea." Carson spoke up. "Also, Max and his sister, Melody, have brought to our attention the need for coats for school children. I suggest we start by figuring out who needs what sizes and go from there."

"I've talked to Melody about the situation and she's going to pass that information on to other teachers," Max chimed in.

"I'd like to say something." Davis Stanford stood and moved toward the door. "I don't think I can do this. Max, I've worked at forgiving you for what you did to my daughter, but I can't allow you to come back to town and start buying yourself into everyone's good graces."

"I didn't think grace could be bought," Max stated simply, allowing for the other man's right to his anger.

"I'm not trying to buy anyone or anything, Mr. Stanford. I'm trying to give back to the community that raised me, to people that I care about."

"Throwing your money around isn't going to make amends, Max. My daughter wore your ring on her finger, thinking she was promised to someone who would put her first. You only put yourself first." Davis brushed a hand through thinning gray hair.

"I know." Max stood up, facing the other man the way he should have faced him years ago. "I'm sorry for hurting her. I have no excuses. I can only apologize. And I'm thankful that Amy has forgiven me. She has a husband who loves her now and a beautiful family. I can't buy grace, Mr. Stanford. It can't be bought. It's a gift. And I hope that as we celebrate the birth of a savior who offers us grace that you can forgive me."

Jack cleared his throat. "I'd like to see if we can return to what is truly important today. We have real problems in our community. Children who are going without. We could get caught up in these old arguments, but I for one understand forgiveness. I have two sons that are here with us today because they were able to forgive me. Davis, you and I have been friends for a long time."

Davis laughed at that. "Not that long, Jack. You weren't very likable until Isaac moved in with you and you had to make changes."

"I guess that's the truth," Jack acknowledged, knowing that his son claiming him as a father almost twenty years ago had changed things for him. "I don't want to get in the middle of this feud, but I'd sure like for us to put it aside so we can do what is best for the community. If that means taking some of Max's hard-earned money, I'm willing to overlook his past sins."

Davis scrubbed a hand over his face. "I'll stay."

But he didn't say he would forgive.

Max sat back down. A hand touched his arm. Without thinking, he covered it just briefly with his own. He slid his gaze to meet Sierra's and, although she didn't smile, he saw understanding.

She struck him as someone who'd had her share of hurt. He, on the other hand, had caused his share of pain. He didn't expect mercy from her, he expected caution. Because he had a history of letting people down.

He didn't want to add her to the list.

The meeting ended with Jack asking Max to continue with the coat drive. He had the resources to bring in donations from outside the community.

Sierra would continue keeping everything organized, making sure the event went off without a hitch. Jack had no doubt she could and would make it happen.

Everyone got up to leave and Max had every intention of following the crowd. However, when he got to the doors to leave, he found himself turning back.

"What are you doing?" Isaac asked, like he was Max's conscience.

"I'm going to talk to Sierra for a minute."

"About the coat drive?" Isaac asked.

He'd never been one to lie. Even as a teen, he'd always owned up to his actions.

"Nope." He settled his hat on his head.

"She's like a sister to me, you know."

"How is Daisy?" Max asked, because he hadn't seen the youngest West sibling in years, not since Jack's wife had hightailed it out of town with her three kids in tow. Not Isaac. He didn't share the same mom as the other West offspring.

"I wouldn't know. Daisy doesn't have much to do with

the rest of us. She has a little clothing store in Tulsa. But don't change the subject. We're talking about Sierra."

"Yeah, I kinda gathered that. And I guess I don't know what to tell you. I'm staying here. I'm talking to Sierra."

"If you hurt her, you'll have to answer to a lot of folks in this town," Isaac warned him.

"I can take care of myself," Sierra stated as she walked out of her office, a cup of tea in hand.

Max noticed she didn't always drink the tea. It might be her way of finding calm. As if to prove him right, she lifted the cup and inhaled.

"Yeah, you can take care of yourself." Isaac shot Max another dangerous look. "Max, I'll be catching up with you later."

"I don't doubt it."

Isaac left. Max took a deep breath and faced the woman he had no right to. He told himself he shouldn't feel a thing. A wiser man would walk away now, before he got tangled up in something that might be hard to leave behind when it was time to go.

"Why are you still here?" she asked.

"Not a clue. I just didn't want to leave yet."

"Did you hurt Amy Stanford?" she asked, taking a seat on the bench outside her office.

"Yes, I hurt her. Looking back, we were way too young to be engaged. We were high school sweethearts and childhood friends. It seemed right to ask her to marry me. She's glad I showed my less than trustworthy self because she went on to marry a pediatrician. She has a good life now with a man she loves, who loves her to distraction. I've never loved anything to distraction, except my family and work."

"I think you're too hard on yourself. You're a good man, Max."

He sat next to her, keeping some space between them.

She didn't completely trust him and wasn't completely comfortable with his proximity.

"It isn't you," she said after a few minutes. "It's the past. You know how the past is. It has a way of sticking its nose into the present. Isaac doesn't have to worry about me getting hurt. I don't allow anyone to get that close."

"Afghanistan?" he asked.

She let out a long breath and closed her eyes. "Yes, and I don't talk about it. It's taken me three years at Mercy Ranch to realize I am whole, alive and I have a future."

"It's taken me less than a week to realize you're a remarkable woman."

She gave him a quick look. "No, I'm not."

He could argue that point but he knew she'd never concede. She was remarkable. He'd never met anyone like her and he wanted to know her better.

Which is why he shouldn't have stayed. He got up to leave and she stood, too. He was tall and she was average height, coming to his chin. When she looked up at him with golden hazel eyes, he wanted to kiss her. Just once, to see if it would be everything he thought it might be.

Instead he took a step back because he knew her fears. And he knew his. If he'd met her years ago, maybe things would be different. But right now they were two people in two different places in their lives.

"I'll see you Thursday," she said, stepping away from him.

"Yes, Thursday." He walked away.

It wasn't easy to do. He couldn't remember the last time a woman made him want to stay. It had been years. Or maybe it had never been.

What was it about this woman, the one who constantly pushed him away, that made him want to get closer?

As he got in his truck he told himself it was the fact that she kept herself just out of reach. *We always want what we can't have.* It was as simple as that.

Chapter Six

Sierra stepped out of her vehicle then reached in for the container of cupcakes. Her stomach roiled a little as she closed the door and faced the single-wide mobile home where Patsy Jay lived with her children. She could see them peeking out the windows, watching her.

Socializing was not her thing. Children were also not her thing. Or so she kept telling herself. They were like tiny soldiers armed with sticky fingers, difficult questions and hugs. They surrounded a person, leaving no room for escape.

The door opened. Patsy stood there looking frazzled, tired and yet happy.

"Come in, we're not too scary." She smiled big, pushing a stray hair back from her face. Even with dark circles under her eyes, Patsy was pretty. She probably wasn't much older than Sierra.

"Of course you aren't scary." Sierra stepped forward, carrying the huge container of cupcakes. Too many cupcakes, she realized, but she hadn't been able to stop.

"What do you have there?" Patsy asked as Sierra made her way up the off-kilter steps, moving to avoid a broken board.

"Cupcakes. A lot of cupcakes," Sierra said.

"Oh, the kids will love you." Patsy took the container and glanced toward the end of the driveway, past the few other trailers on her end of the park.

"That must be Mr. St. James," Patsy said unnecessarily as the truck was pulling to a stop behind Sierra's SUV.

"Must be." Sierra stepped inside the trailer, telling herself it didn't matter to her that Max St. James had arrived.

It didn't matter that he had taken her by surprise the day of their committee meeting. She'd wanted to sit with him longer, sharing stories. She never shared stories. What was she thinking?

Linnie moved from the window to the middle of the small room, her dog at her side. The big shepherd took up a lot of space in the small living area that was already crowded with two sofas, two end tables and a playpen in the middle, where Patsy's youngest played with a rubber giraffe. The other child, a boy who appeared to be only slightly younger than Lennie, ducked behind a footstool and peeked out at Sierra. She wiggled two fingers at him and he raised a hand to do the same. He giggled and waved again.

The living room shrunk even more when Max walked in. He didn't look her way, not at first. He removed his jacket and his cowboy hat. His forest-green-brown eyes were covered by sunglasses that he removed as he stepped farther into the room. He brushed his hand through his unruly chocolate-brown curls.

The two of them made eye contact with the barest of smiles, then he turned to greet the children.

Max squatted in front of Linnie and the little boy who had clambered out from behind the footstool to stand next to his older sister. Max spoke to them and then, without hesitation, pulled the baby from the playpen and held him in his arms.

Sierra remembered that she'd brought sprinkles for the cupcakes. She dug into her purse and pulled out the Christmas-colored candies. "I thought the children might like to decorate the cupcakes. I know Christmas is several weeks away but it's always fun to make things festive."

"They would love that." Patsy took the jars from Sierra. "That was so nice of you. We always try to do Christmas cookies. It's a tradition. But I've been so busy with work and school, I'm just not sure when we'll get around to it. I still need to get my tree out of the shed in the back so the kids can decorate it." Her eyes flooded with tears. She wiped at them, appearing to be half-angry at herself for crying. "I'm so sorry, it's been almost a year and the waterworks still come at unexpected times. I didn't expect to be doing this alone."

Sierra searched for the right words, the kind Kylie would have said in a moment like this. She didn't want to offer platitudes. This woman—Patsy—she needed real help, not a passing comment about things getting better.

"You don't have to apologize," Sierra said. "I can't imagine what you've been through. But I can tell you, waking up each day, taking steps forward and doing what needs to be done, even when you don't want to, those are the signs of someone who's going to make it. I'm sorry, I'm not good at this. I haven't been through what you're going through so I can only speak from my own experiences."

Patsy grabbed her in a tight hug. "Oh, Sierra, thank you. That is actually what I needed to hear today. Just to know that I'm going to survive. One day at a time."

Patsy grabbed a tissue and wiped her eyes. "I'm such a watering pot. But thank you both for coming and allow-

ing me to do this. I think that sometimes people are afraid
to impose. They don't want the poor widow to cook for
them. But I need to do this. I need to do something normal, to feel like I still have my life and…just, thank you."

"You're welcome," Max said. He was still holding the
baby boy. Although not as closely. "I hate to be a downer,
but this guy is not smelling too great. I don't change dia-
pers. But I'll be happy to go out to the shed and get your
tree and other decorations, if that would help."

"I would be so thankful." Patsy took the baby from
him. "Oh, Johnny, you are definitely stinky."

"Do you need help?" Sierra called after Max as he
headed for the front door of the trailer.

He grinned, as if he knew she was escaping to fresh
air. "If you want."

Sierra stopped midway through the living room where
Linnie had plopped down on the floor with her brother.
They were watching an educational cartoon on TV, arms
around one another. As Sierra stepped around them, Linnie looked up and smiled. The child's hand reached for
Sierra's. The big dog sprawled out next to the children
raised his head to give her a warning look.

Sierra touched her fingers to Linnie's hand.

"I'll stay here unless you need me," Sierra said.

Max glanced back, saw her with Linnie and grinned.

"I think I can manage," he told her.

Her breath hitched and she tried to ignore that smile.
It was the smile of approval, of promise. And she didn't
deserve it.

Still, when he left, she settled on the floor with the
children, as if she did it every day. She pretended it didn't
bother her that the dog licked her hand or that she might
possibly be sitting on a chewed-up cookie.

Patsy called out that she was going to the bedroom, so they wouldn't all have to deal with the toxic diaper.

"Johnny's smelly," Linnie said to Sierra.

Sierra's head jerked around at the softly spoken words and Linnie grinned at her.

"He is a little," she agreed as Linnie returned her attention to the television.

The front door opened. Max placed a tub down on the floor. "I found Christmas."

She remained sitting on the floor with Linnie. "I hope you didn't bring any spiders or mice with you."

His smile teased. "I'm not guaranteeing anything."

Linnie giggled.

"I didn't bring any spiders or mice into the house. But I found the tree and decorations. I'll be back in a minute with another tub."

"We'll be here," Sierra informed him, turning her attention back to the cartoon.

Max returned a few minutes later with another blue tub, this one full of decorations. He pushed his way into the living room and nearly tripped over the dog. The animal gave him a warning look as he stretched and moved to the other side of the room.

"Don't worry, bud, I'm not about to harm your family."

The dog didn't look convinced. Instead it found Linnie and sat next to the child. She didn't look as if she needed the protection tonight. Linnie, her brother Teddy and Sierra were all at the table, dozens of cupcakes lined up, waiting to be decorated. He watched as Linnie dipped a finger in icing and took a lick.

Patsy shrieked and grabbed the cupcake. "Linnie, no tasting. You can't share cupcakes that you've been eating."

"Sorry, Mama." Linnie went back to decorating, sprinkling red and green stars, silver bells and sugary glitter on the icing.

Patsy hugged Johnny close and leaned to kiss her daughter. "I love you."

Linnie nodded but didn't stop decorating, placing the sprinkles and glitter in just the right spots.

"Thank you so much for bringing the cupcakes," Patsy said to Sierra as she handed Johnny to Max. She smiled at him. "If you don't mind holding him, I'll get the lasagna out of the oven."

The child smelled decidedly better now, so Max took him, holding him on his right side as he picked up red sprinkles.

Sierra guided three-year-old Teddy's hands to dust green sprinkles over a white-iced cupcake. Max waited until she looked up before he lifted his cupcake and took a big bite. Johnny grabbed his hand and pulled the cupcake toward his own mouth, tasting the icing.

"Hey, you'll ruin your dinner," Sierra scolded.

"Nothing can ruin my dinner. I could eat a dozen of these cupcakes and still eat lasagna."

"If you did, you wouldn't be so—" She cut herself off and her face turned a shade of pink that rivaled the sprinkles she'd brought for the cupcakes.

He lowered his voice. "I wouldn't be so what?"

It was a dangerous game he played with the wedding planner.

"I need to get these kids washed up for dinner." Patsy swooped in, took Johnny and told the other two children to follow her. "We'll be right back with clean hands and faces."

"I'll clean up this mess so we can use the table," Sierra offered.

"No hurry." Patsy giggled as she walked away.

"So what?" Max asked Sierra again.

"So…"

"Nice?" he asked. "Tall? I get that from my father. I also run and work out several times a week. My condo has a gym. And a pool."

"Stop," she said as she focused on his mouth.

She grabbed a napkin out of the holder on the table and started to wipe his mouth. Just as quickly she pulled back, as if she had been caught by surprise.

"Where?" he asked.

She handed him the napkin, then pointed to the spot on the corner of his mouth.

"Here?" He wiped the wrong side.

"Stop." Her eyes lit with mirth.

"You might have to help me," he told her.

Sierra wasn't a woman who played flirty games. He should have known that. She started gathering up the cupcakes, moving them to the kitchen counter. He liked the idea that she might be attracted to him. What would she say if he told her he might be attracted to her prickly self? He guessed she wouldn't like being called prickly. She also wouldn't like it if he told her she smelled like sunshine.

Years ago, Melody'd had a pet hedgehog. He remembered trying to pet it once. It had jumped, hitting him with sharp quills, warning him to stay away. Sierra reminded him of that hedgehog.

He grabbed several cupcakes and carried them to the counter, setting them next to the growing number she'd lined up in a disposable aluminum baking dish.

"I'm sorry for teasing you," he whispered to her.

"It's okay. I kind of stepped right into it. And I don't

think you need me to tell you what your best attributes are."

"Now you have me all aflutter."

She laughed, the sound husky and all Sierra. "Really? 'Aflutter'? How very Victorian maiden of you."

"It's better than telling you I'd like to kiss you and getting punched in the face. That would be awkward. Especially since we have to work together on the committee and on Melody's wedding."

Silence reigned between them for a long minute. Then she turned away from the cupcakes she'd been arranging. "Yes, a kiss would be awkward. You're making this difficult."

He pointed to himself. "Who? Me?"

She rolled her eyes at that. "Yes, you. You're making my life very complicated."

"I didn't mean to."

Patsy returned, talking louder than necessary as she came down the hall with the children.

"What can I do to help?" Sierra asked Patsy.

Soon she was putting dishes on the table, pulling plates and flatware from drawers. Max herded the children to the living room until they were called to dinner.

They sat at the small table and joined hands. Patsy asked him to say the blessing. As he did it, he realized that this moment, simple as it was, felt right. In the past five years his life had changed drastically. He'd gone from family dinners to fancy dinners in cities far from home and family. He'd eaten at exclusive restaurants in New York City and Paris. His life had changed and he thought he'd changed, too. Seemed like he was still the kid from Hope who liked to team rope and drive his truck down back roads with the windows down.

Tonight, dining on lasagna, with Linnie eyeing the

French bread on his plate and Johnny in his high chair drooling more than he ate, was one of the best meals he'd had in years. Sitting across from him, Sierra made small talk yet looked very uncomfortable, as if this was the furthest thing from normal to her.

When Linnie reached for Sierra's bread, Sierra handed it over.

"Sierra, you don't have to do that!" Patsy turned a bright shade of red. "Honestly, Linnie!"

Linnie ate the bread. Then slipped a bite to the dog beneath her chair.

They all pretended not to notice.

After they'd finished eating, Max helped clear the table. The dog, suddenly his best friend, remained close. Obviously he was used to the table scraps. Max offered him a piece of bread on the sly. The dog grabbed it and ran to the living room.

"Do you want me to set up your Christmas tree?" he asked Patsy.

Linnie grabbed his hand and tried to pull him toward the living room.

"Would you? That would be wonderful." Patsy wiped at a drop of water on her face. "We'll be right in to help. And thank you for this evening, and again, for coming to our rescue."

"Just being neighborly," Sierra said in her reserved way. "That's what I've learned living in Hope, that everyone here is a neighbor and they help each other."

"Yes, you're right. People have been so good to me since…" She hesitated. "Since the accident. I don't know what I would have done without our neighbors."

Max left the women to talk because he suddenly felt out of place. The children followed him and helped as he pulled the pieces of the fake tree out of the tub. They weren't a lot of help in putting it together.

Sierra appeared several minutes later and started to pull out strands of Christmas lights, checking to make sure they would light up when plugged in. Sierra was relaxed, joking with the children, sharing stories with Patsy.

But the stories were all about her recent past. As if her life began the day she arrived at Mercy Ranch.

Teddy grabbed his attention away from the puzzle that was Sierra Lawson. The little boy held up a snowflake decoration with a family picture in the middle.

"Do you want to put this on the tree?" Max lifted the boy and, with pudgy, clumsy toddler hands, Teddy managed to hang the ornament on a branch at the top of the tree.

Patsy glanced their way and he saw tears in her eyes. It was their first Christmas without her husband. Max loved his family and could not imagine losing any of them. They'd lost his grandfather when he'd been young, too young to remember how that loss had felt.

At the end of the evening, Patsy looked around her trailer and smiled as she hugged her children. "I can't begin to thank you both for this night. Again, I thought I was going to repay your kindness and instead the two of you have stepped in and changed our lives with your friendship. It doesn't just look like Christmas, it *feels* like it."

"You've changed our—my life, as well." Sierra stumbled over the words, giving Patsy and then her children quick hugs. "I've enjoyed being a part of your family tonight."

Soon Max and Sierra were standing on the porch with

the bare bulb making a halo of bright light that illuminated their way down the steps and to their cars.

Patsy waved a final goodbye and closed the door.

The air was cold with an early December bite. Sierra pulled her jacket a little closer and then dug in her purse for her keys. She pulled them out and then tried to hide the pink-haired troll keychain.

"Did you get that in your kids' meal with chicken nuggets and apple slices?" he teased.

She held the troll out in her hand. "If you must know, I've had it since I turned sixteen. A friend gave it to me. It actually squirts glitter."

She gave the troll a squirt and glitter flew from its nose. And then she laughed.

What kind of woman carried a glitter-spraying troll keychain? He never would have suspected the serious Miss Lawson of something so juvenile. He wouldn't admit it, but he felt a little bit of a crush on her as she stood there smiling up at him, the glittery troll in her hand.

"Don't look so surprised. I was a teenager once. I just... This friend wanted me to laugh..."

"Because you didn't laugh often?"

"I guess not." And just like that, she shut down again. "I should go."

He walked with her to her car because it seemed the right thing to do. Actually, it seemed like the only thing to do. He took the troll keychain from her hand and unlocked the door with a push of a button. Then he stood there, not sure what to do. Sierra stood next to him, her reserve pulled around her like a cloak. He glanced from her to the glitter troll in his hand and, before he could second-guess, he squeezed it and glitter wafted into the cold night air. It sparkled in the security light and then fell over her head like a gentle rainfall.

For a moment, she looked shocked and then she laughed. "Did you seriously just do that!" she said.

"I did." He was surprised by her laughter and that he wanted to kiss her good-night. But he knew that it would be a mistake to kiss her. They were standing under a full moon on a cold December evening and pink glitter clung to her hair and cheeks.

Grabbing hold of his common sense, he pulled back, but not before he brushed a bit of glitter from her cheek. His hand lingered there just briefly.

"I should go," she said in a way that made him wonder if she felt the pull between them, too. The look in her eyes said she did.

"Yes," he agreed. He opened the door of her car and she took back the glitter troll.

He closed the door and stepped away from the car, away from the crazy mix of emotions she'd stirred up in him. As she drove off, he told himself it had been the moonlight and glitter, nothing more.

He wasn't so sure.

Chapter Seven

The wedding chapel looked like a Christmas forest and not a Christmas wonderland. Next to Sierra, Glory made a "hmm" sound.

The younger woman had returned the previous day and Sierra was glad to have her back. She was a good worker with a keen eye for detail. She was also a decent roommate.

"I don't like it," Sierra said for the second time.

Glory pushed back her fall of curly blond-brown hair and studied the situation through her thick glasses. "It needs something. Definitely not more trees!"

"Yeah, a bulldozer. Maybe a lumberjack. It's just too much. It needs less of everything."

"Could we move some of the trees out? Maybe with a less crowded forest, we could make it more artistic," Glory suggested.

"The bride's family ordered two hundred trees for the chapel." Sierra sighed as she surveyed the mess. "I have an idea. We leave the trees at the back, by the stage. We place the rest around the edges. Maybe have a forest of trees at the back of the chapel."

"Maybe. And then move the extras to the reception

hall. A forest of trees in the reception hall makes more sense. Receptions should be all about twinkling lights, stars overhead."

"Okay, we're going to need help with this."

"Help with what?" The voice came from behind her. She hadn't even heard him approach she'd been so focused on figuring out the tree problem.

"Hi, Jack." She smiled at the older man as he stopped next to her. "We can't see the forest for the trees."

"I can see how that would be an issue." He shook his head. "Why can't people just walk down the aisle of a church the way they used to do?"

"Well, if they did, the Stable would be out of business."

He laughed. "Guess I can't argue with that. So what do you need help with?"

"We have to clear the forest. I know the family had an idea about the number of trees, but this is ridiculous."

"It certainly seems that way. I'll send over a few men."

"But that isn't why you wandered this far from the house, is it?" she asked. "Do we need to go to my office?"

"Not really, but I would like to sit down, and I know you have the best coffee on the ranch. Even if you don't drink the stuff."

"I'll send Glory to start a fresh pot of coffee and we can go sit in the lounge."

Glory darted off without waiting for instructions.

The younger woman, although she'd grown up in a dysfunctional mess, loved her job and loved proving herself. While she wasn't the most effusive boss ever, Sierra hoped Glory knew she was appreciated. She made a mental note to tell her more often. Because people liked to be told they were doing a good job.

The lounge was a sitting room across from Sierra's office. The chairs in the lounge were comfortable. A big table in front of a fireplace gave families a place to look over different wedding themes, colors and decorations.

Jack settled himself in one of the wingback chairs near the window.

"What's up?" she asked.

He steepled his fingers and studied her in such an intense way, she squirmed. Jack, founder of Mercy Ranch and a Vietnam veteran, served as a mentor, a boss and a father figure to all the veterans who lived on Mercy Ranch. When he studied a person like that, it made you wonder what he saw or what he wanted.

"Are you doing okay?" Jack started. "I think you are. You look happy. I like that look on your face."

"I'm doing well, Jack. No problems."

He paused as Glory entered with a cup of coffee, setting it on the table next to him. She looked from Jack to Sierra and back to Jack. "I'll go find some work to do. Yell if you need anything."

She closed the door behind her as she left.

"You didn't come all this way just to see how I'm doing," Sierra guessed.

"Actually, I did. We haven't talked in a while. You're always busy and you rarely come to Sunday lunch."

"I'm sorry. I should. I've been meaning to."

"Don't fib. I know you're uncomfortable with big family events. You're happiest in your kitchen, alone, making cakes or cupcakes that keep us all happy."

"Guilty as charged."

"Have you talked to your parents lately?"

"I have. I'm fine with them, Jack."

"Sierra, I know working at the Stable isn't your dream job. I'm here because I want you to start thinking about your dream. This is something to keep you busy. It isn't your future, though. And I think you need to find it. Find what makes you happy. You're ready for your next step."

"Jack, I'm happy here. I don't have any desire to leave Mercy Ranch." She hesitated, her heart sinking at the thought. "Do you want me to leave?"

"No, no. This is your home. Always will be. You're one of my kids. No, I just want to know that you're pursuing your dream. The wedding venue has given you some mettle, some backbone. But it isn't forever. Start thinking and praying about what God has in store for you next."

"I'll do that. Thank you, Jack."

"You don't have to thank me. I don't know where I'd be without you kids keeping me going."

She glanced out the window at the winter landscape, the brown grass, the trees devoid of leaves, the icy-gray sky. Why did clouds look so different in the winter?

"Sierra, if you need a break, let me know. I know the Christmas event is a lot to put on you…"

She continued staring out the window as she tried to come up with an excuse or explanation for her hesitance.

"It isn't that I don't want to." She shook her head at that. "No. The the truth is, I don't want to take this on."

Jack started to speak but she held up her hand.

"I don't *want* to, but I *need* to. I could hide away in the safety of Mercy Ranch. I know my faults, Jack. I know that I tend to shut people out. It's always felt safer than having to deal with people. But I'm learning something about myself, and isn't that what you wanted? I'm learning that I do like people. I like to help others. I think I told myself I don't like people or crowds because it felt safer than getting involved and getting hurt."

"I know it won't be easy to figure this out." Jack reached for her hand, clasping it in both of his. "But you're one of the strongest women I know."

"Thank you." She blinked against the sudden sting of tears in her eyes. "I mean it. For everything, thank you."

He patted the hand he held. "Oh, let's not fool ourselves. Most of the time when you walk away from me muttering, you're not being thankful."

She laughed at him. "You're right about that."

He sat back again. "One more thing."

"Oh, what's that?"

"You're not going to like it, but I want you to trust me. Kylie has a dog for you. Bub. He's a Labradoodle."

"I told her I don't want a dog."

"I know what you've told her. But I have a theory."

"What's that?"

"You don't want a service animal. You don't want a dog that labels you as injured because you think that will take away your strength. It will be admitting to human frailty."

"Ouch," she said.

"Yes, I know. The first time I walked into a twelve-step program, I felt the same way. A stronger man would have kicked the habit on his own. I finally had to swallow my pride and confess that I had an addiction and needed help."

"I'm not…"

He waved a hand at her. "You're not an addict, not to pills or alcohol. But to control. You are addicted to control. You don't like to lose it. You want to rule everything in your life, including your emotions."

"You're being particularly honest today. It's painful."

He winked. "I like to make the most of the time I have on this earth. Take the dog, Sierra. Put a collar and leash on it. Just let it follow you around. There's something else, too."

She buried her face in her hands. "I'm afraid to ask."

"I think you're afraid to love a dog or to let the dog love you. And if you love a dog, what doors that might open up."

"If you stop talking, Jack, I'll agree to take the dog."

He pushed himself to his feet, leaning heavily on his cane. "Mission accomplished. You're going to work on finding your dreams. And Kylie will bring your dog to you."

She followed him out of the Stable. "Hey, Jack, you know that control thing I like so much?"

"Yep."

"You're the master."

"That I am, Sierra. But I only use my power for good, not evil."

She kissed his cheek. "Thank you. For caring about me."

"I want you happy and settled."

"I hope by 'settled,' you don't mean married. I plan weddings, Jack. Other people's weddings."

He headed out the door. "I just want to see you smile more often. You do that for me and we'll be even."

He didn't look back. Isaac was waiting to help him into the ATV they drove around Mercy Ranch.

She smiled but it felt more like a grimace. Jack wanted her to work with Max St. James. He wanted her settled. She knew Jack well enough to know what he was up to. She also knew enough to keep herself from being dragged into his plans.

All of this stuff about being settled, happy and finding her dreams was very suspicious.

As she headed back to her office, her phone dinged. She pulled it out of her pocket and groaned as she read the text.

Max St. James wanted to meet at Holly's Diner.

* * *

Max reached for the door to Holly's, remembering back to when he was a kid and this was the only place in town for a burger, a milkshake, a piece of pie. Now, because of Jack West's expanding influence, there were other options. A restaurant attached to the resort at the edge of the lake, a tearoom in the old hotel on Lakeside Drive.

The crowd inside Holly's proved that competition didn't necessarily hurt an established business. Sometimes more options meant more business for everyone. The renewed vitality of the city had brought in a decent tourism trade.

He scanned the crowd, searching for Sierra.

It had surprised him that she'd agreed to meet.

"Hey, Max, looking for someone?" Holly, a few grades behind him when he'd attended school in Hope, headed his way.

"Sierra Lawson?"

"She's in the back room. She didn't say anything about meeting you, though." Holly gave him a questioning look that bordered on suspicious.

"She's a private person," he responded, wondering if he would always have to explain himself here, in Hope.

"I promise, she knows I'm meeting her." He sighed.

Holly gave him a wry look, pursed her lips together like a mother hen guarding her chick, then beckoned him to follow. She led him through the main dining room to a small room in the back.

"This is new," he commented.

"I wanted a room for meetings and parties, something more private." She nodded toward Sierra sitting near the window. "I'll be back in a minute with water and menus."

"Thank you." And then he stood there for a foolish moment, caught in a strange web of curious attraction.

Sierra's head was bent as she perused something on her phone. Rays of sun shifted through the window and caught strands of gold in her auburn hair. She looked up, catching him in that moment, and a smile faltered on her lips.

"I'm sorry I'm late," he said as he took a seat across from her.

"Not a problem. I've been working on details for the Christmas at the Ranch event. I'm assuming that's why you wanted to meet?"

"No, not really. But we can discuss it if you want. I know there are still a lot of details to take care of."

She lowered her gaze back to her phone, a hint of red spotting her cheeks.

Holly returned with water and menus. "Do you need a minute?"

"I know what I want," Sierra said. "Chef's salad and your vinaigrette dressing."

"Burger and fries for me." Max handed back the menus.

"When the others get here, send them back." Sierra reached for her water, all innocent, like she hadn't just dropped that information out of the blue.

"We're meeting with others?"

Sierra stirred her water with the straw. "I invited Kylie because she has her finger on the pulse of the community. Also, our pastor's wife, Tish. We are going to discuss decorations, the schedule for the event, workers needed for preparations and for helping the day of the event."

Suddenly everything became clear to him. "You don't want to be alone with me," Max said.

She sat back, her eyes widening. "I'm not sure what that means. I'm here, aren't I?"

"Yes, you are. But why did you agree to meet me when it's obvious you don't want to be here alone with me? Not that we're alone. There's a whole diner full of people."

She trembled and reached again for her water. "It isn't you."

"I want to think it isn't." He pulled off his cowboy hat and sat it on the chair next to him. He caught her gaze lingering on his face. "My grandparents were Christians in Iraq. They made a decision to immigrate to America, where they knew that they could have freedom to worship. They knew in America there were opportunities, not only for their faith but for jobs, for freedom, for a future without ever changing governments."

"I understand that."

Her face had paled, her freckles standing in stark contrast against her warm, ivory complexion. He regretted his hastily spoken words.

"I'm sorry." He spoke softly, aware that she was scooting back in her chair. If she planned to leave, he planned on stopping her. He didn't want her to walk away, not from him or from this conversation. Not now, when he thought he finally might be finding the missing pieces to the Sierra Lawson puzzle.

"I might have had a brief moment when I first saw you," she admitted, her eyes downcast. "But it wasn't you, it was everything. The helicopter…"

"Tell me," he encouraged, keeping his tone soft.

She shook her head. "No. That isn't why we're having this conversation. I have to go."

"Don't." He stood to follow her.

Her back was to him but he saw her shoulders stiffen and then she turned. She closed her eyes for a brief moment and he immediately understood. The noise from the main room.

"We can close the door," he offered. He wanted to reach for her. He had the strangest urge to hug her, to comfort her. Those weren't typical thoughts for a man used to constant motion, working eighteen-hour days, rarely even stopping to talk to his secretary.

"Please," she said.

He nodded once and then closed the door. "Better?" he asked when he returned to her side.

"Better. It isn't always like this, but today my nerves are on edge and the noise is too much."

"How do you plan weddings? Because that seems like it would be living in constant chaos?" He felt a twinge of anger with Jack West for putting her in that position.

She grimaced but it almost appeared to be a smile of sorts. Without explanation, she reached in her purse and pulled out earplugs. "When it's too loud, I put these in. People don't notice. It doesn't block voices really, just the background noise."

"Nice." He laughed as she shoved the case back into her purse.

"You are very nice," she added. It took him by surprise. "I mean that. And don't look so shocked, I'm not always rude. I do have some people skills and I can see that you're a kind person. You're good to your family, to small children and to the elderly. That says a lot about you."

He put a hand to his heart. "Wow, I'm blown away."

She laughed at the reaction. "Well, don't let it go to your head."

"I won't. But I must admit, I wasn't always a nice person."

"So I've heard, but I typically ignore gossip."

"It isn't gossip. Every bit of it is true. The drunk and

disorderly destruction of public property, the miserable way I treated Amy. I lost my scholarship and my dad had to pay legal bills and college. He shouldn't have, but he wouldn't give up on me. Even when I didn't appreciate it. That's why I owe them so much. I owe them everything."

"You're blessed to have parents like them. And I don't think they did it with any thought as to how you would pay it back."

"I'm aware of that. When I look at my family, I see the sacrifice and I think of what Jesus meant to us. His birth. His death. His resurrection. He didn't ask for payment, only acceptance. I'm the prodigal son."

Her gaze darted to the doors that had opened while he talked and she smiled. "There's the rest of our group."

She hurried forward to hug Kylie and then the slightly older Tish Stevens. The three returned to their table, talking about Christmas plans, baking and how to finish the planning of the Christmas at the Ranch event in time to pull it all off.

Kylie shot him a questioning look and he shrugged. What could he say? He had hoped to have lunch with Sierra alone and now realized that maybe it was better to meet with a group.

The women were discussing food to be served and setting up the committee for serving and cleaning up. They had various sign-up sheets at the local churches for people who would help set up, hand out the gifts and clothes, and clean up afterward.

At one point Sierra looked across the table, caught his gaze and mouthed that she was sorry. He nodded because he understood. She had a pink troll that sprayed glitter, earplugs to block out the chaotic noise of a wedding reception and dark shadows under her eyes. She was complex, funny, scared, sad—and the first woman to ever touch his heart in a way that frightened him.

Chapter Eight

"Do you think we should use the angel or the star for the top?" Glory called out to Sierra from the living room, where the younger woman was busy decorating the Christmas tree.

Sierra closed her eyes and counted to ten, careful to hold the frosting so that she wouldn't squeeze it all out and ruin the birthday cake she was making for Patsy's little boy Teddy.

Glory had been firing questions at her nonstop for thirty minutes. Garland or beads? Clear lights or multi-colored lights? Red and gold decorations or multicolor?

Sierra hadn't put up a Christmas tree in years. Not since her sophomore year in high school, the year her mother had left her father. The year her parents had fought, knocked down the tree, and her dad had landed himself in jail. She definitely hadn't scrapbooked the family Christmas photos or kept ornaments to remember those times.

But that was then, this was now. Be present in the life you have now, Kylie had encouraged. Jack wanted her to find herself, her dreams. The life she had now was a good life, even with the occasional flashbacks, the memories, the old baggage that she was working to unpack. She didn't need to keep carrying around all of that stuff.

"Sierra?"

She set the tube of frosting on the counter, wiped her hands on a dish towel and wandered into the living room. Standing on a step stool, Glory placed the star on the top of the tree. Her baby, Cara, was in the playpen with a light-up toy that played music. The little girl, now more toddler than baby, grinned up at Sierra and held out pudgy arms.

"I don't think so, you droolly little thing." Sierra leaned down to run her fingers through wispy blond baby curls.

"She wants you to hold her," Glory said with her sweet Oklahoma accent and a big grin. Her large black eye-glasses slid down her nose and she pushed them back up.

"How do you know that? She's grinning the way she grins when she wants food, her mommy, a diaper change and when she sees the cat outside."

"She's holding her arms out to you."

Sierra shook her head. "I came in here to give you some much-needed tree-decorating advice. It looks to me as if you already decided what to put on top of the tree."

"I was just trying to get you in here. I thought it might be fun if we decorated together." Glory hopped down from the step stool, her paisley skirt swirling around her legs. Her blue-gray eyes twinkled from behind her glasses.

"Tree decorating isn't my thing," Sierra told her. "I'll hold Cara."

"No, she doesn't need to be held. She's having fun playing and she might take a nap. She was fussy at church today."

"She's never really fussy," Sierra said. "She's actually pretty happy and easy to be around. For a baby."

Glory didn't look at all offended. "You like her and you know it."

Sierra gave the baby another look and Cara grinned, exposing tiny white teeth and dimples in her cheeks. "I do like her, Glory."

"So multicolor or white lights?" Glory grabbed up the two boxes of lights. "It'll be easier if we both help do this."

"You're determined, aren't you?"

"I am. No one should dislike the holidays this much, Sierra. It isn't healthy."

"I have bad memories," she admitted.

"Then we'll make new ones," Glory said with all of the pluck and optimism of someone young and starting a new life for herself.

Glory had been through so much in her childhood. Her parents in and out of jail on drug charges, getting addicted herself, losing her baby. Yet, here she was, optimistic and finding a path to happiness for herself and her baby girl.

"I'm sorry," Glory said. She bit down on her lip and cast her gaze away from Sierra. "That wasn't nice. We all have our own stuff and we all have to work through it in our own way. And I know that I haven't been through anything like what you've been through. I've never been to war, or taken captive."

"Isn't there a verse about Him coming to set the captives free?" Sierra offered, a way to change the direction of the conversation.

Glory's smile returned. "Yes, there is. In Luke." She closed her eyes and thought a moment. "'The Spirit of the Lord is upon me, because he hath anointed me to preach the gospel to the poor; he hath sent me to heal the brokenhearted, to preach deliverance to the captives, and recovering of sight to the blind, to set at liberty them that are bruised.'"

"You have it memorized?" she asked as the baby behind her chortled then let out a squeal. Sierra turned and lifted the little girl from the playpen.

"I memorize a lot. One of my professors said I have an almost photographic memory. I do forget some things." Glory held up the lights again. "So, which ones?"

"You don't give up, do you?"

"Another thing that more than one person has said to me." Glory gave her an unabashed grin.

"White lights and multicolor decorations." Sierra shifted Cara to her other side because sometimes her right side, her right leg, felt stiff with too much carrying or walking. Not as often now, but it still happened from time to time. She sat in a nearby chair, still holding Cara.

"What are your plans for Christmas?" she asked Glory as she watched the girl untangle lights and plug them in.

"I'm going to be here at the ranch. My dad..." She shrugged. "Well, he's in jail again and my mom moved to Oklahoma City with a friend. I'd prefer it here, anyway. Do you have family?"

"I do, but they're in Ohio and I'm not fond of arguments. My mom is remarried and my dad is still himself, so I'll stay here and have dinner with the Wests."

"Someday I want to get married and have a big family with a lot of kids. I want to have holidays where everyone sits at the table together and we all laugh and smile. I know for some people that's normal. I'd like for it to be my normal." Glory held up the lights, giving Sierra an expectant look. "Are you going to help me?"

"I'm going to help you." She put Cara back in the play-pen. "You can have all of those things, Glory."

"What about you?"

Sierra took the lights from the younger woman. "I'll start at the top on the back and wrap it around. You grab it and bring it back to me."

"That wasn't really an answer," Glory noted as she took the string of lights to pull them around the front of the tree.

"No, you're right. It wasn't. I don't have answers. I think I'll probably always live at the ranch and I'll always prefer my own company to others."

"Why not get married and have kids?"

"Because that isn't everyone's journey. I'm content in my life here. Maybe complacent," she admitted. "But I'm happy. I've had my fair share of bad relationships shaking up my happiness. I'm not going to let that happen again. Can we just decorate the tree now, please?"

Sierra thought about what Jack had said to her, that he wanted her to find her dream. She could only think of one thing she really loved and that was baking. She was most happy when she baked.

"Can I ask one more question?"

Sierra groaned. "Must you?"

"I must," Glory said with a sly grin. "What about Max St. James? I mean, he's not just any man and I can't see him making anyone unhappy. I mean, he has his own a helicopter!"

"Max St. James?" What would make Glory bring him up? She gave the other woman a questioning look.

"I don't know. I think he's handsome and he has his own business. He's good to his family. Also, the two of you look cute together."

"No thanks. I'm really very happy with my life the

way it is. I don't want to add anything that might upset the balance."

Sierra started hanging ornaments on the tree. Red, silver, gold, blue. She watched as Glory took more time, carefully placing each in a specific place. She was thoughtful and kind, even though she hadn't been shown a lot of kindness in her life.

"I have to get something from my room," Sierra said. "You finish up here."

"Wait, you promised to help me," Glory called out. "You're not getting out of this."

Sierra called back, "Keep decorating and I'll be right back."

Sierra returned a few minutes later with several wrapped gifts. Glory and Cara deserved gifts under the tree.

"You've already been shopping? I thought you didn't like Christmas." Glory stepped down from the step stool.

"It isn't that I don't like the holiday itself. I don't like some memories attached to the day. But I do like you and sweet little Cara. I bought the two of you a few gifts. No big deal."

The look on Glory's face made Sierra want to disappear. "Don't cry!" she ordered.

Glory blinked and sniffled. "Sierra, that's the nicest thing ever. I thought our tree would look empty until I could get to the store, but you're a step ahead of us as usual."

"It isn't a big deal. I like you and Smelly Britches more than you know."

"Oh, we know. And we love you, too."

Sierra placed the gifts under the tree. "I'm going to let you finish decorating the tree. I need to get this cake to Patsy for Johnny's party tomorrow."

She tiptoed from the room. Cara had fallen asleep, her pudgy hand under her flushed cherub cheek. She was sometimes smelly but always sweet, and Sierra felt an odd rush of emotion at the thought of that little girl and her mother. She swallowed past the tightness in her throat and hurried back to the safety of her kitchen.

On her way out a few minutes later, she stopped to see the progress of the decorations. Glory had moved on to hanging wreaths and setting out dust collectors. Sierra smiled in spite of herself. "There's a roast in the slow cooker if you get hungry before I get back."

"Oh, thank you!" Glory paused mid-decorating and waited, glancing around the room as if waiting for a comment or compliment.

Sierra followed the younger woman's gaze, a little overwhelmed by the amount of Christmas that had exploded inside their apartment.

"You don't like it?" Glory asked.

Sierra made sure it she smiled at the other woman.

"I think it's perfect." And she meant it.

Glory gave her a quick hug. "I know you don't like hugs, but thank you for decorating the tree with me. I didn't want to do it alone. It makes it more like family if we do it together. And thank you for cooking."

Sierra stiffened in Glory's embrace but then relaxed. "I enjoyed it, too."

Sierra's car was parked under the carport a short distance from the apartment. As she opened the door to place the cake box on the floorboard of the back seat, she heard someone call her name. She looked up and saw that it was Kylie.

Kylie waved for her to join her at the dog pen.

"No!" she called back. "No, I don't want to see cute puppies or kittens."

Kylie laughed, the sound carrying across the distance. "Kittens don't live in the kennel. They live in the barn. Please come over here and met Bub."

Curiosity got the better of her. "Bub? Why would you name a dog Bub? I've heard Shep, Buddy, Rascal. But Bub?"

Kylie led the dog from his run and when she raised her hand, the dog sat. He was a scruffy-looking dog, dark brown with a wiry face that was almost comical. "You sure he's a Labradoodle?" Sierra asked. "Because he looks like a werewolf."

Kylie put her hands over the dog's ears. "Shh! You'll hurt his feelings."

"I wouldn't want to do that because he has enough going against him. But really, if you ask me to say he's cute…"

"He *is* cute."

"A face only a mother could love," Sierra said. But she let the dog sniff her hand then ruffled the wiry but somewhat soft hair around his face. "What a mess."

"He loves storms." Kylie leaned to talk to the dog. "Don't you, Bub? And you love to cuddle and hang out in the mornings with a cup of coffee and toast. He likes crowds of people."

"I'm not giving the dog my toast and you know I don't drink coffee."

Kylie smiled up at Sierra. "He's special, our Bub is. He's blind in his left eye, so he obviously can't be a guide dog."

"Kylie, I just…" The dog with the dark chocolate eyes looked up at her, his mouth open in what appeared to be a doggy grin.

"He would love an owner for Christmas. I've been working with him at my house. Jack kept him for a couple of months. If you decide you really don't want him, I can find him a home. But it might take a few months."

Sierra balked at that. "If I take this dog, he stays with me."

Kylie blinked a few times. "I wouldn't take him from you."

"No, of course you wouldn't." She shook her head and tried to laugh it off. "I don't want to get attached and then have something happen."

"Of course not. If you take him, he's yours."

Sierra squatted in front of the dog and they stared each other down. She blinked first. Of course.

In the distance she heard horses running. She gave the dog a firm pat on the head and stood. "I have to go."

But then she saw Max. He rode across the arena, Isaac just ahead of him on a big gray.

Kylie followed her gaze. "Oh, team roping."

"I see." Sierra checked the time. "I have to go. I'm taking a cake to Patsy."

"Bub?"

Sierra looked down at the dog. He had moved closer to her side, leaning in slightly. "Why is he doing that?"

"Dogs sense things."

She shook her head. "What do you think he's sensing?"

Kylie shrugged a little. "I guess that you need him."

Sierra dropped a hand to the dog's head. She didn't need him. He looked up at her with chocolate eyes that matched his chocolate fur. She wanted him, though. She wanted his friendship, his sweetness. She'd never really wanted a dog but now, everything felt different.

"All right. He can move in tonight."

Kylie did her best to look serious and not amused.

"Great. I'll leave his run unlocked and you can pick him up when you get home."

"Thank you," Sierra said. And then she gave her friend a quick embrace. "Really. Thank you."

She headed toward her car but got distracted by the men on horses. She might have convictions about remaining single but she wouldn't deny there was something about a man sitting on a horse that was very distracting. Even if that man was Max St. James.

Especially because the man was Max St. James.

Max saw Sierra out of the corner of his eye. She was above average in height and she ate up the ground at a quick pace when she walked, that auburn hair catching the sunlight. He didn't want to admit it, but his heart kicked up a notch at the sight of her.

He'd been working nonstop for the past ten years, building something out of nothing and missing what was important. He told himself that was all there was to this. He was finally remembering that there was life to be lived and he had to take time to live it.

Suddenly the steer was out of the box and Isaac was fast behind it. Max's horse shot forward, nearly losing him in the process. He had to lean in fast and grab with his legs to keep from having a bruised ego and a backside to match. His hat flew off and he couldn't get the rope up to grab the steer's legs.

He pulled in the rope and circled around to get the hat that had fallen off his head.

Isaac was laughing so hard he could barely stay in the saddle. He pulled off his hat to smack it on his leg, laughter still rumbling deep in his chest.

"What in the world was that?" Isaac shouted at him as the laughter faded.

"Sorry, I got distracted. It happens."

"Distracted by what?" Isaac asked.

"The, uh, steers over there. You going to dehorn those things anytime soon?" Max looked toward the pasture in an effort to get Isaac to look that way.

Bullheaded as usual, Isaac looked in the opposite direction. He spotted Sierra and slid his gaze back to Max. "Don't blame the steers. That isn't what had your flummoxed."

"Who says 'flummoxed'?" Max asked.

"I do. It's the perfect word." Isaac sat back in his saddle and hooked his right knee over the saddle horn. "You are flummoxed. Bewildered. Confused. Muddled. It happens to the best of us. And it usually has something to do with a woman."

"I'm not flummoxed."

Isaac unhooked his leg and slid his booted foot back in the stirrup. "Yep, you are."

"I need something to do this week. If you're going to work those steers, I can help. I'm assuming that's why you've got them up here."

Isaac shifted his attention to the fifty-some head of cattle in the pasture closest to the arena they were using. "Yeah, I thought we'd work them while the weather is decent. They're predicting a cold December."

"Let me know when and I'll be there."

"I'll let you know." Isaac turned his horse. "Shall we try this again? Maybe this time you could focus on the bell?"

"Yeah, I will."

Together they moved the steer back to the chute. A few of the ranch residents were standing behind the chute in the pens. They helped get the steer situated as Isaac and Max positioned themselves.

"You ready this time?" Isaac asked with a wink. "Don't be nervous, but she's watching. And Sierra never watches. She joins us on a trail ride from time to time, but the whole cowboy thing isn't her cup of tea."

"How can I get you to shut up?" Max mumbled.

"You're talking to my bad ear. Did you say you think I'm the best?"

Max shook his head and readied himself, making the arena his focus and not the woman watching. He did not notice that the breeze caught her auburn hair, lifting it around her face. He did not notice that she pushed that hair back and held it so that she could watch them.

"Hey, get your head in the game!" Isaac yelled.

The buzzer rang and the steer bolted from the chute. Max and Isaac broke loose from the boxes on their horses. Isaac's lasso caught the horns and he tightened the rope on his saddle horn to bring the steer to the left. Max's rope circled the steer's back legs. His horse took a step back, tightening the rope. Someone in the background yelled, "Four seconds."

"Yeah, that's how it's done." Isaac shook his rope loose from the steer's head. Max did the same from the back legs. Unharmed, the steer trotted away.

"I have to ask her a question," he told Isaac.

"Really? Things have gotten that serious."

Max shook his head and rode off.

Sierra cocked her head to the side when she saw him heading her way. "Nice roping," she said.

"Thank you. It's been a long time. And you saw one of our better attempts. I'm glad you came over because I was given a mission and my grandmother threatened bodily harm if I come back without talking to you."

"What's that?"

"She's baking tomorrow evening and she'd like for

you to join her. It's early for Christmas baking, but she wants to take some things to Tulsa."

"I would love to join her. What time?"

"Five o'clock tomorrow and you can help fix dinner." Max steadied his horse. "Sorry, that might be more than you were wanting to do."

"No, that's fine. Of course I want to."

"You look a little unsure."

She hesitated. "Honestly?"

He gave a slight nod. "Sure."

"I'm not used to big family dinners. It scares me a little. If you haven't noticed, I'm not a social butterfly."

"Don't worry, we're harmless. Noisy but harmless."

"Okay, I'll be there." She backed away from the fence. "You boys have fun. Try not to break anything."

"We'll try," he said.

He watched her walk away and then turned back to the men who were all waiting for him. Isaac arched a brow but didn't say anything. Good thing because Max didn't have any answers. As a matter of fact, he had a lot of questions.

Chapter Nine

Sierra didn't typically sleep in. This morning she had. She'd also discovered something she disliked more than oversleeping. She didn't like being woken up by a wet nose nudging her hand. She considered ignoring him but knew that would mean suffering the consequences. That in mind, she got up, found Bub's leash and headed for the side yard to walk him.

They were sniffing flowers and trees, or the dog was, when Kylie joined them. She looked far too chipper and Sierra wasn't quite ready for that.

"Looks as if the two of you are fast friends."

Sierra shot her a warning look.

Kylie gave her an unrepentant smile. "Someone hasn't had her morning tea yet."

"I overslept."

"Wow, that never happens."

"No, it doesn't. What am I supposed to do with him while I'm out?" Sierra looked down at the dog on the end of the leash she held. "I'm gone a lot, you know?"

Kylie put on her calm face that she used to negotiate or bring a peaceful solution to a situation. "The point to having Bub is that he's your companion. You take him with you everywhere, to work or to church."

Sierra shook her head. "People will stare. I go through life trying not to draw attention to myself and now you want me to drag this poor animal with me?"

"People will be drawn to him, yes. But you will adapt. You're very good at adapting. And you've been around these dogs, even helped me with them. You know what he can do for you and you also know how to handle him."

Bub moved to her side, signaling he'd finished his business. They headed back to the apartment.

"What if I visit a home that isn't dog friendly?"

"Most people are going to understand. And it isn't as if you're taking a dog that you're going to turn loose and he's going to rampage their house. He's your companion. He'll be sitting next to you. Most importantly, he's there when you need him."

Sierra studied the wiry-faced dog that continued to grin at her. She thought of all the times in the past few years when a flashback or anxiety attack had taken her by surprise. They always happened at the worst possible time in the worst possible place. She considered how the situation might have been helped if she'd had a dog. "Okay, I will do this."

"Good. I know you won't be sorry."

"But he might be," Sierra said. "And now I have work to do. I'll see you later." She headed for the door, Bub at her side.

"Where are you going?" Kylie asked as she hurried to catch up.

"Somewhere," Sierra responded with a smile, knowing it bothered Kylie to be left in the dark. "And thank you, for Bub. I'm sure I won't forget to feed and water him."

"He'll remind you."

"I won't forget to take care of him," Sierra assured her friend.

"Okay, well, I'll see you later." Kylie headed for the main house.

Sierra watched for a moment, then she headed inside to get a few errands finished before she left.

After lunch she left the house, the dog at her side. She opened the back door of her SUV and motioned him inside. He complied, jumping in and taking a seat as if this was what they'd always done. "I can't believe I'm doing this," she told the dog. His ears perked up and he grinned. "Must you always be so happy? Do you understand what is going on? I'm not a dog person. I'm not even a people person."

Bub gave a soft woof.

A dog that talked back. She shook her head and closed the car door. On second thought, she opened the door and gave him a pat on the head that had him moving his head to gain more attention.

"Glutton," she accused as she closed the door.

It was a ten-minute drive to the St. Jameses' ranch. White fences bordered the property line that ran parallel to the paved country road. The gravel drive led to an older, two-story farmhouse, with a wraparound porch. It was obvious renovations had recently occurred. New windows gleamed, reflecting the sunlight that had peeked out from behind the wintery clouds that held on since sunrise.

She parked near the unattached garage and got out. A woof from the back seat reminded her that she had a dog who would also like out of the car. She opened the back door and Bub jumped out. He shook himself from head to tail and then sat next to her.

"You'd better never leave me, dog." She held out her hand and he nuzzled it.

"Hey, you made it." Melody crossed the yard, pulling on a jacket as she did. Her smile was wide and welcoming.

"I made it."

"You have a dog!"

Sierra looked down at the animal. "Yes, I do."

Although Kylie had promised the animal would be a pet, inconspicuous she had said, he was not just a pet. His harness was bright blue and emblazoned with the words "Service Animal."

"I think that's awesome. I've always wanted a Labradoodle."

"I feel somewhat awkward expecting people to allow me to take him into their homes. I don't know if you have allergies or cats or an extreme dislike of dogs."

Melody touched her arm. "Sierra, bring your dog inside. Nonni and Mom are waiting for you. It's girls' day. We're going to cook and bake. Dad and Max went to Tulsa for the day, buying more cattle. I'm not sure when they'll get home."

"If you're sure?"

"I'm sure." Melody looped her arm through Sierra's and they headed across the lawn.

They climbed steps to a porch on the side facing the driveway and walked around to the front door.

"It's a beautiful home," Sierra said as they entered through the front door into a living room decorated for Christmas. The tree in front of the window twinkled with lights and music played softly. They walked through that room then a formal dining room and into a large kitchen.

"We love this old house," Melody responded. "And even more so since Max did the renovations."

Nonni and Max's mother, Doreena, were at the counter together. Side by side, their shoulders touched and their heads tilted as they shared a private conversation.

"We're here, you two." Melody walked up behind her mother and kissed her on the cheek while wrapping her arms around the other woman. Doreena St. James twisted around to give her daughter a quick hug.

Sierra stood back from the warmth of the family, a little envious of their affection for one another.

"Sierra, we're so glad you agreed to join us." Doreena greeted her and then she spotted Bub and her smile grew. "Oh, isn't he beautiful?"

Sierra glanced down at the dog. "Really, you think so?"

"I do. He's very handsome. May I pet him?"

"Oh, of course." Sierra raised her hand and Bub sat next to her. "Kylie West gave him to me and today is our first day together."

Doreena fondled the dog's ears and then petted his back. "I love him."

After giving Bub attention, Doreena washed her hands. "We're going to fix one of our favorite rice dishes for dinner and then we'll make the pastries with dough that my mother made earlier today. Would you like to slice the steak for me? I'll cook the eggplant and tomato while you do that. We layer the ingredients and then put the rice on top. Think of it like an upside-down cake."

"I'd love to help," Sierra said as she turned on the water to wash her hands.

Nonni walked up behind her and began to explain the process of slicing the steak and how it would be layered with the tomatoes, potatoes, onions, peppers and eggplant with the rice on top. And then it would be inverted to make a layered dish.

"It sounds wonderful," Sierra told Nonni and the older woman patted her arm. "What is it called?"

"It's called *maqluba*. I think you will like it very much."

Sierra washed her hands after cutting the meat and watched as Max's mother cooked the vegetables and removed them from the pan.

"Of course she'll like it." Melody poured a cup of tea and handed it to Sierra. "Max said you don't drink coffee, so I made tea. I hope you like peppermint."

"Thank you, I do." Sierra took the cup and told herself not to get caught up in teenage emotions about a man who took the time to tell his sister that she liked tea.

They moved on from the meat dish to a salad and a pasta. The conversation flowed, as did the laughter, coffee and desserts.

"Oh, there are the boys." Nonni turned from the window. "They're unloading cattle. They'll be hungry when they get here. That Max, he is always working. He needs a wife to tell him to slow down and enjoy life."

Melody grinned over the top of her cup but she didn't comment other than to wink. Max's mother laughed a little but continued to work on the meal. It seemed to be a conversation they were used to.

"Max won't marry until he learns to make time for a woman," Doreena commented. "And he shouldn't. He needs to learn to prioritize."

"Because women don't like to sit and wait for a man who forgets his promise to take them out," Melody added. "Not that he's terrible, but forgetfulness and women isn't a good combination."

Sierra realized the last thing she wanted to discuss was Max and dating. The whole idea made her strangely uncomfortable. Nonni had started the pastries. She'd placed the walnuts, sugars and possibly cardamom in a skillet with butter. Sierra moved to her side to watch.

"This is the filling for the pastries," Nonni explained. "Will you roll out the dough?"

"Of course. I'd be honored."

For the next thirty minutes, the four women worked together in the kitchen. Sierra pretended she wasn't waiting for Max to walk through the back door.

Max's sister, his mother and Nonni were wonderful. They laughed as they worked together in the kitchen. They told stories and teased one another. They were a family.

She was included but she wasn't a part of their circle.

The back door opened and Max stepped inside. Sierra's breath eased. He hadn't noticed her, so she stole a quick look. Or two. Maybe three. She watched as he pulled off his jacket and hung his cowboy hat on the hook near the door, all the while he talked cattle with his father.

"We have company," Doreena warned. "So mind your manners, both of you."

Max jerked around, as if he'd forgotten that he'd issued the invitation for her to join them.

Max's father, Aldridge, smiled at her. "Well, if it isn't our wedding planner. Hello, Miss Lawson."

Her gaze connected with Max's but she responded to his father. "Nice to see you, Mr. St. James."

She froze, unsure of what to say next.

Max moved to the coffeepot. "Did they make your tea?"

"Yes, thank you."

Just like that, she felt out of place, like she didn't belong. Or maybe she'd always felt that way and she'd convinced herself she felt a part of this group of women. "I've had a wonderful time baking with you all. But I should go. I have…" She hesitated. "Stuff. I have stuff to do."

"Stay. Please," he said. His hand on her arm was warm, his expression kind. No, more than kind. The look in his chocolate-brown eyes hinted at something and it frightened her, that look. It spoke to something deep inside her, something unfamiliar. A longing for someone.

She wanted to go but she didn't. Her heart yearned to be here in the midst of this family.

And it took her by surprise.

Max had forgotten that Sierra would be joining them. It had taken him by surprise, walking in and seeing her in the kitchen with the women of his family.

She faced him with her own astonishment. Her eyes widened and she wrung her hands in the apron tied around her waist. His gaze settled on the smudge of flour on her cheek. Someone cleared their throat and he realized he was staring. Still, he couldn't drag his attention from her softly freckled cheek and that dusting of flour.

Nonni clapped her hands together. "Okay, let's eat!" she said. "We have so much to do this evening. We have to decorate the tree, finish our pastries and Max must teach Sierra our wedding dance."

"Oh, I don't think so…" Sierra started. "I'm not much of a dancer."

"Oh, nonsense, we can teach anyone to dance. Come, come, let's set the table. Sierra, will you fill glasses with ice? For you, I've made the American tea."

"Oh, thank you." She looked around, a little lost, maybe overwhelmed.

"I can help," Max offered. After all, he was the one who'd invited her here. He'd put her in this situation where she looked as much like a cornered rabbit as any person he'd ever met.

Nonni's brow scrunched. "Max, you never help in the kitchen."

"Nonni, I'm never here to help. I'm very proficient in the kitchen."

She gave him a look that older women know how to use so effectively. Right before they dropped the bomb. "Oh, yes, of course. You're a bachelor, without a woman to take care of you. I see that you must cook or eat at restaurants." She shook her head as she looked at Sierra. "I pray for this one to find a wife but what woman wants a man who works all of the time."

"Nonni, if you're praying, maybe you should trust that God can handle my bachelorhood."

She laughed at that, her dark eyes twinkling. "Yes, smart one, I do trust God. He always has a better plan than mine."

"I love you, Nonni." He kissed her cheek then opened the cabinet to show Sierra where the glasses were kept. They were shoulder to shoulder and she smelled good, like baked goods, floral perfume and tea.

"You invited me but you looked surprised to see me here," Sierra said in a soft voice as they pulled glasses from the cabinet.

"I forgot, but I'm also surprised you actually came."

"I surprised myself," she admitted, handing him glasses that he filled with ice.

They soon carried the glasses with ice to the table. After setting a glass at each plate, he found himself next to her again. This time he couldn't resist. He wiped the smudge of flour from her cheek. She blushed furiously.

"You had a little something there," he said.

"And you waited until now to tell me?"

He glanced down at the dog that had joined them. "I was somewhat afraid of your guard dog."

She smiled, the gesture making her hazel eyes seem lighter. "I don't think he knows how to guard. He's a companion. That's all."

"I'm glad you have him."

She reached to pet the dog at her side. "So am I."

His family joined them, bringing dishes from the kitchen. Then they stood around the table, joining hands. His father blessed the meal and they all sat down to eat. In typical St. James fashion, the conversation resembled a tennis match with comments volleying back and forth.

Sierra was mostly silent, taking it all in, Max noticed.

After dinner, Nonni stood. "Your mother and I will wash dishes and you young people may do as you wish. Sierra, before you leave, I have pastries to send home with you."

"What young people are you talking about, Nonni?" Max asked as he started gathering plates.

Nonni pointed at him. "You. Melody. Sierra. She is a guest and we have worked her too much."

"I enjoyed myself," Sierra assured his grandmother. "I got to spend time with your family and learned new recipes. Thank you for including me. I do have to be going soon."

Nonni gave Sierra a quick hug. "I'll get a container of pastries for you to take home. Max will show you the house while you wait."

Max agreed to guide Sierra through the downstairs of the house. The living room was newly decorated. While it was the living room of his childhood, the remodeling process had changed it. The memories hadn't changed. Of past holidays…family gatherings… The night the police had brought him home after he'd crashed his car into the school… His father's disappointment… His mother's tears…

"Seems like the Christmas decorating has already started," he stated unnecessarily.

There were candles, a Nativity scene and other decorations already scattered about the room. A sprig of mistletoe had been left on the table. Melody's doing, he was sure.

"Have you been able to reach out to your contacts about coats?" Sierra asked, dragging his attention from the mistletoe.

"I have," he said. "There are several organizations willing to help buy coats. I actually meant to talk to Melody about that. I think she and other teachers, as well as some local church groups, are taking down sizes, ages, names. I'll get that list in the next few days and send it to those groups so they can begin to buy the coats. They want to include hats and gloves, also."

"That's wonderful!" Melody exclaimed as she entered the room with her mother and grandmother.

Nonni immediately handed a container of pastries and one of leftovers to Sierra. That was his nonni, always trying to feed people.

"The timing's going to be tight, but I think we can pull it off." Max told his sister, his attention slipping to Sierra because she was moving toward the door after hugging his mother and grandmother.

"I should go. But thank you all for including me." Bub seemed to pull a little on his leash and gave the door a meaningful glance.

"I hope you'll come back soon," Max's mother said, giving Sierra another quick hug.

"I'd like that." Sierra's hand was on the doorknob.

"I'll walk you to your car," Max offered.

"You don't have to."

"I want to." He reached past her to open the front door.

On the porch, she stopped. "What are you doing?"

He knew what she meant so he didn't bother pretending he didn't. They were merely two people on a committee together, thrown into each other's lives by a series of events that no one could have predicted. He was only in Hope for the holidays. And yet he found himself doing things he couldn't have predicted. Like taking time to walk this woman to her car.

"Max?" Her softly worded question tugged him back to the present.

"I'm not even sure."

"At least you're honest. I need to walk Bub before I put him in the car." She headed down off the porch.

They allowed the dog to lead them around the yard. The moon was bright, lighting up the lawn, the fields, the barns. Bub sniffed the air and tugged a little on the leash. Sierra issued a soft command and he returned to her side.

They stopped at the far edge of the lawn. Somewhere in the distance a coyote howled. Bub gave a soft warning bark.

Sierra paused to look up at the inky sky that held millions of stars. The air was cold and she shivered.

Max patted the mistletoe in his pocket.

"I saw you take it," Sierra said.

"What?"

"The mistletoe."

He studied her face and he saw that she was unsure. He didn't want to take advantage.

"I did take the mistletoe," he confessed. "And then I realized that was cheating. When I kiss you, Sierra—and I will kiss you—I want it to be mutual. I want to know that it's what you want, too. I want you sure of whatever it is that's happening between us."

"I saw you take the mistletoe, cowboy," she whispered, "and I'm still here." Her hand touched his cheek, her skin cool, her gaze searching.

He didn't bother with the mistletoe. He leaned in, brushing his lips against hers. She kissed him back, her hand sliding to the nape of his neck. Bub growled low, bumping against Max's leg as if to disrupt things.

Sierra smiled into the kiss and then pulled away, cool air taking up space between them as she moved farther from him.

"Thank you," she said.

"Thank you?" He couldn't remember ever being thanked for a kiss.

"For this night, for your family, and for reminding me that I am definitely a woman and I'm alive. And I can be held by a man and not fear it. You have no idea what that means to me."

"You are definitely alive and I want you to know, I will never do anything to hurt you."

"Not on purpose," she said.

"I hope not even by accident."

His words pulled a sad smile from her and she kissed his cheek. "I have to go now. Please don't walk me to my car and please know that I'm not upset with you."

"Okay."

"Good night, Max."

Then she was gone and he stood there in the circle of bright moonlight wondering at the gift she'd just given him and worried that he would definitely hurt her.

That was the last thing he wanted to do.

Chapter Ten

The room was dark and she couldn't breathe. Sierra fought against the unseen enemy and struck out. Then she was awake and a cold nose pushed against her face. Bub crawled up against her and she feared she'd been hitting at the dog. He didn't seem at all hurt by her. He rested his head on her shoulder and she wrapped her arms around him, finding comfort in his presence. Her breathing slowed. The nightmare faded.

Bub stayed next to her as gray light began to ease its way into the room, signaling the start of another day.

"You know you're not supposed to get on the bed," she reminded the dog. Bub whimpered and crawled closer.

"Don't push it, Bub." But she wrapped her arms around the dog, allowing him to do his job for just a moment longer. And it worked. Her fears evaporated and she knew that this was her room in Hope, that she was not alone in a prison cell. "I think we're going for a run."

Bub looked skeptical.

A few minutes later she was ready and Bub, after a bowl of kibble and some water, appeared to be eager to go. She left a pot of coffee and a container of blueberry muffins for Glory.

Cool December air greeted her as she stepped out the front door to stretch. Bub snuck a look at the front door as if he was rethinking this run with her.

"I promise I'll make it up to you," she told him as they started down the driveway. "Just a short run."

She needed the reality of the cold air, the pavement and the sun coming up on the eastern horizon. She needed to watch the morning sky change from gray to pink, pale orange, lavender and then blue. In the light of a new morning she found hope. His mercies were new every morning.

Morning meant she was alive. Morning held the promise of another day, another opportunity. Each day was a gift.

"I'm alive, Bub."

The dog gave her a quick look but he seemed to know that he was in for the long haul. He paced himself next to her as they headed out on the open road with nothing but fields on either side.

Cattle, curious by the presence of a human, moved to the fence row to watch her jog past. Bub let out a low woof. She laughed at the dog, at the cattle, at her own flash of optimism, of joy. She hadn't expected to feel so good, not after the nightmare.

Maybe it had to do with Christmas being less than three weeks away. Or maybe it was because the nightmare hadn't been real. New memories were edging in. She kept running, just the sound of her feet, a panting dog, a tractor in the distance as someone moved hay for their cattle.

Max St. James had kissed her. She'd kissed him back. She tried to remember the last time she'd wanted that man to kiss her. Last night she'd definitely wanted to be kissed by Max.

As a teen she'd wanted so desperately to be loved. She'd found nothing but heartbreak. For the past ten years she'd avoided relationships, choosing to focus on herself rather than to find a man to fill that emptiness. And now, here was Max.

She kept running. The town was a good twenty-minute run from Mercy Ranch. It was a run she'd made several times a week for the past few years. Especially when the nightmares crept in, when the past threatened to steal her peace. The peace she'd found at Mercy Ranch.

In the distance she could see the intersection that led to town. She slowed her pace, giving her heart time to slow. She took the right turn onto Lakeside Drive where it was obvious Christmas was weeks away. Star-shaped lights had been hung from the streetlamps. Stores were decorated. The church had set up their Nativity on the lawn.

The city had added a new sign: Embrace Hope in Hope.

A car slowed behind her. She glanced back and smiled at Kylie. She slowed to a walk. The car pulled up next to her and the passenger window lowered.

"You're out early," Kylie said. "Going to Holly's for breakfast?"

Sierra stopped walking to catch her breath. Bub sat next to her. She had a dog. A very tired, panting dog. Loyal, he was also very loyal for sticking with her on this run.

"Can I go to Holly's with Bub?"

"Of course you can. He's a service animal. Are you okay?"

Sierra straightened, stretched, ignored the question, stretched some more. After a deep breath, she nodded. "I'm good. Meet you at Holly's."

Kylie gave her a careful look. "You don't want a ride?"

"Nope. I need to cool down."

Sierra and Bub walked the block to Holly's. There were already cars lined up in front of the building. Cars, trucks and even a tractor. She'd grown up in Cleveland, so she was still amused by the sight of a tractor in town, parked in front of the local café. Occasionally there would even be a horse or two tied up to a light pole.

She entered with Bub at her side. No one really seemed to notice the dog. A few people waved. Someone called out to her that she made the rest of them look bad. Kylie waved from a table near the window. Isaac's wife, Rebecca, was with her. Sierra didn't dislike Rebecca but she didn't know the other woman that well, even though they had been roommates for a time when Rebecca had first shown up in Hope to start a salon and day spa. Sierra didn't share stories or do girl-talk the way most women did. It was just easier to keep to herself.

Rebecca pushed a full glass of water across the table for Sierra. Sierra sat down, reaching for the water. Bub stretched out on the floor, probably wishing for his own glass of ice water. She wondered if Holly would bring the dog a bowl of water.

"Good to see you, Sierra, but I have to go. I have an early perm at the salon."

"See you later." Kylie stood to hug her sister-in-law.

"Sierra, I'll see you later. And I've set out a box at the salon to collect gifts for the Christmas event. Do you want me to bring them to the ranch?"

"Oh, I'm not in charge of Christmas at the Ranch," Sierra clarified.

"But you are on the committee," Kylie reminded her. "With Max St. James."

The last thing she wanted to think about was Max. Or

their kiss. She felt her cheeks heat up and knew she had to be turning a horrid shade of red.

"I'm sorry," Rebecca said. "I didn't mean to put you on the spot."

"You didn't," Sierra said quickly, because Rebecca was kind and helpful and it wasn't her fault that Sierra suddenly couldn't keep her thoughts focused. "I am on the committee and if you want to bring stuff out to the ranch, that would be fine."

"I also have some things for the Lakeside Manor nursing home. Several of my clients have donated small throw blankets."

Sierra must have looked confused because Rebecca continued to explain.

"It's a mess up there with the new management. Gladys Adams is at Lakeside for a brief stay, rehabbing her shoulder, and the staff is under strict orders to curtail the holiday festivities for residents."

"I think I did hear something about that. And didn't Gladys fall off a horse?" Sierra asked.

"I hope I'm still riding horses at eighty," Kylie said with admiration.

"You will be," Sierra said. "So, yes, Rebecca, definitely bring what you have for the Christmas at the Ranch event. And find out about the nursing home gifts because I'd be willing to donate something."

Rebecca left, Holly brought tea and a bowl of water for Bub, took their orders and then left them to talk.

"This wasn't a normal run," Kylie stated after the café owner walked away.

Sierra looked over at a table of men, one being Kylie's husband. Dr. Carson West had been estranged from his father, Jack West, but he'd returned a few years ago and had taken the job as the local physician. Then he'd married his childhood sweetheart. Kylie.

"Are you sure you don't want to join your husband for breakfast?" Sierra urged. Because she didn't want to talk about her nightmares.

"Nah, I see him all the time. How's Bub doing? He seems to be settling in."

"Things are good." Sierra glanced down at the dog. "He crawled in bed with me this morning. I told him he no longer has to sleep on the floor."

Kylie's face split in a grin. "Now, that's what I like to hear. You're letting him do what he's been trained to do. He's such a good boy."

"He is."

Their food arrived. For a few minutes they didn't talk about nightmares, dogs or anything else that might have made Sierra feel uncomfortable. And yet Sierra felt angsty. The kind of angst that had nothing to do with the past and a lot to do with change and the unknown future.

Kylie toyed with the last of her eggs. "Why did Bub feel the need to comfort you?"

Sierra's gaze drifted to the window, to the Christmas-decorated streets, to the church a few blocks away. "Nightmares. It's been a while since I had one so vivid."

"I'm sorry." Kylie cleared her throat. "As your friend, not your therapist."

"Good, because I really just need a friend today."

"Oh?" Kylie asked.

"He kissed me," Sierra blurted out.

Kylie laughed a little and looked around at the other tables. "Bub kissed you?"

"Stop!" Sierra peeked through her fingers, which were covering her face. "You know who I mean."

Kylie became serious. "I know who you mean. And

you think that's why you had a nightmare and also what had you running at zero dark thirty this morning?"

"Yes, that's what I think." Sierra sat back in her chair with a sigh. "I'm acting ridiculous. Just say it. I'm a thirty-year-old woman who should be able to navigate relationships, holidays, emotions. But I'm terrible at relationships. I'm terrible at trusting."

"You're a thirty-year-old woman who was held captive and tortured."

"Shh," Sierra said. "I know my labels. Domestic Abuse Survivor. POW. Wounded Warrior. Veteran. But I am also a survivor. That's how I choose to label myself."

"Even survivors have bad days, Sierra."

"I know that." Sierra briefly closed her eyes. When she opened them, Kylie was studying her, waiting. "I kissed him and I didn't fall apart."

Instead she'd felt the opposite of falling apart. And that might have been what frightened her most of all.

At noon on the Monday after Sierra had visited the St. James family, Max was knee-deep in farmwork. He stood to one side of the corral, the mutt dog at his side as they moved cattle through a chute to give them immunizations, tag the ears and label the newer livestock.

His dad yelled something about a heifer and Max looked up, completely lost. Then he saw her. The dog immediately brought the Angus heifer back to the herd.

"I know you're used to office work," Max's dad called out, "but do you think you could join me here on the ranch?"

Max took his hat off and wiped his hand through his hair. He definitely wasn't the best farmhand. "Yeah, sorry, Dad. I got distracted."

He never got distracted. His dad gave him a look,

shook his head and said something to Richard, the hand they'd recently hired. Both men laughed.

It was no laughing matter. One solitary kiss on a moonlit night had him questioning everything about himself. He never questioned his goals, his plans. College had helped him see the bigger picture. It had changed him from a selfish teenager to a man with a plan to restore everything his family had lost.

And yet he'd never felt it was quite enough. Even now, he couldn't go to the café or to church without noticing the skeptical looks. People doubted his intentions. The other day his sister had asked him if all of this—the house, the ranch, the cattle—was for his parents or to ease his guilty conscience.

Where did Sierra fit into this plan of his?

"You're woolgathering again," Aldridge called out. "We've got a half dozen head to go. And I'd rather not have to take you to the ER."

"I'm on it," Max called back, moving in behind the cattle, the dog staying close to his side. "Easy, now."

The dog whined. The chute closed around another heifer. His dad and Richard worked quickly, the chute opened and the heifer ran across the field to join the rest of the herd.

"What are we doing next?" he called out.

His dad motioned him to keep the cattle moving. "I thought I'd eat a sandwich and then I'm going to fix the fence along the road before we put cattle on that twenty acres."

"I can go get our supplies and we'll be ready to go."

"Sounds good to me. We can finish up here if you want to load the truck."

Another heifer moved through the chute. "Yeah, I can do that."

Max walked across the yard to the big barn that had been on the property for several decades. He and his sisters had played in that barn as kids.

The dog his dad had adopted from the shelter ran across the yard to join him. He gave the mixed-breed, wiry-haired dog a pat on the head and opened the truck door to let the animal jump in.

"Going with me?" he asked the dog.

The dog barked.

"Yeah, well, you're not driving, so get over." Max pushed the dog so he could scoot behind the wheel. He needed to back up to the side door of the barn and load new posts, fencing and tools.

His dad joined him after the truck was loaded. He had a thermos of coffee and a bag of what looked like cookies.

"Where's Richard?" he asked his dad.

"He's going to work on the barn repairs. The spot on the roof that leaks, the floor of the hayloft. All of the little things that haven't been kept up."

"Sounds good. Let's go build some fence."

"Got everything?"

"I think so. It's been a while since I fixed fence. I think I did miles of it as punishment when I was a kid, so I doubt I've forgotten the basics."

His dad grinned as he scanned the supplies. "Yeah, you've got it all. I have to tell you, it feels pretty good to be out here working this land again."

"Dad…" Max started, "I want to thank you. For everything."

"Max, I don't have a lot of regrets. I would have regretted not giving my kids the best I could give them. Selling this place put us in a position to help you get your life together. It got you and your sisters an education. It wasn't without sacrifice, for any of us, but it was worth it."

"I put you through a lot."

His dad patted the dog that had jumped into the back of the truck. He grinned at Max. "Yeah, you weren't exactly easy. But you turned out okay. Now, let's go build some fence. We could spend all day worrying about what's already done, or we can spend the day on what matters right now."

They drove down to the section of fence that needed repairing. For the next few hours they pounded in new posts, pulled fence, replaced fence and talked. They also took time to rest, sitting on the tailgate of the truck and drinking from the thermos of coffee Aldridge had brought from the house.

"You know, son, sometimes a man has to be willing to take a chance."

The non sequitur surprised Max. They'd just been talking about fencing and cattle.

"I think I've taken plenty of those," Max said. "I've started two companies from scratch and bought into another."

"Not those kinds of chances, not that you haven't done well. I think you have to take a chance and let yourself get invested in a relationship. Maybe ask a woman out to dinner and show up, not just physically but emotionally."

Max poured coffee into the extra mug. "I just haven't found a way to balance my time between work and a social life. It gets complicated."

"I guess someday, if the right woman comes along, you'll make time."

"I guess I will." But he didn't see that happening anytime soon.

As soon as the thought crossed his mind, another thought took its place. Sierra Lawson. She'd been on his mind way too often.

They were loading supplies back into the truck when a car pulled up on the highway. Patsy Jay got out and he could see that she was worried. Max and his dad headed for the fence and she met them on the other side.

"Is everything okay?" Max asked.

"It's just…" Patsy bit down on her bottom lip. "I can't believe I'm doing this. I left a message on Sierra's phone, but she hasn't called back. I just got a call from my mom. She lives in Grove and she's going to the ER with chest pains. I have older neighbors and younger neighbors, but no one I really trust to watch my kids. I was heading that way but I saw you and…" She let the words trail off. "This is so embarrassing. I don't want you to think the wrong…"

"Now, don't you worry about a thing," Aldridge said. "We're friends, Patsy. We don't mind helping with your kids."

"Are you sure?" Patsy looked from his father to him.

Max gave a quick nod but he had to admit, this was pretty far outside his comfort zone. He'd never seen himself as a babysitter. Patsy's three children were cute but they also required food and diaper changes. He could clean out a stall, doctor a calf, but kids were a whole different ball game.

"Might want to call Mom and see if she's on her way," he told his dad.

"Yep, got her on the line."

Max managed to smile for Patsy, who looked like she was holding on by a thread.

"Bring them up to the house and we'll meet you there."

She hurried back to her car and her children. Max returned to the truck, where his dad had already gotten behind the wheel.

"Good practice for you." Aldridge grinned at Max.

Max climbed in and slammed the door to make sure it latched. "You need a new farm truck."

"That doesn't make any sense at all," his dad told him. "This old truck has a lot of miles left on it, and you don't bring a new truck to the field to get bumped around by angry bulls, scratched up by rambunctious steers. Nah, I'll keep this old truck till it falls apart."

Patsy met them at the house. She had the back door of the car open and was helping her kids out of their car seats. Linnie grinned when she saw him and headed his way holding Teddy's hand. Patsy lifted Johnny from the infant seat and held him close, the diaper bag on her other arm.

"I just got a call from Sierra and she said she'd come right over to help." Patsy shifted her youngest son and Max reached for the child. "I appreciate this so much. You understand, I don't know how long I'll be gone…"

"Go, and don't worry about a thing, the kids will be fine and we'll be fine taking care of them."

His dad shot him a look that Max tried to ignore. He put his hat on Teddy's head and herded the children toward the house while Patsy called out last-minute instructions that he would probably forget.

An SUV pulled off the main road onto the drive. Sierra. She'd wasted no time coming to the rescue of Patsy and her children. He ignored the "gotcha" look on his dad's face.

Chapter Eleven

Max stood at the edge of the lawn, a baby clinging to his neck and Patsy's toddler and preschooler clinging to his legs. She parked, waved at Patsy, who was departing, and smiled at the man whose expression begged for help. She sat there for a moment willing herself not to laugh. She'd had a long day, though, and this situation brought some lightness to her mood that she hadn't expected.

She grabbed her purse and got out of her car. Bub hopped out and stood next to her. Sierra rested her hand on his head and led him around to the back of the car where she could better see the situation at hand.

Max's dad was trying to convince Linnie to take his hand. He had bent down to her level and was telling her a story that had the little girl grinning, but she didn't appear to be ready to let go of Max. For a moment he touched her head, a reassuring gesture.

Her hero.

Sierra couldn't help it. A man who would volunteer for this was a man worth knowing.

"A little help, please?" he said.

She chuckled, not moving from the rear of her car. He was too adorable standing there in his cowboy hat, dust-covered jeans and scuffed-up boots with those three children clinging to him.

There was something about a cowboy holding a baby.

Then her heart did something strange. It felt like the first flower of spring just beginning to open after being tightly closed up against the cold of winter.

"Sierra?"

She closed the distance between them finally. His father had gone on to the house, thinking Sierra must have experience. Because wouldn't most women her age?

"Johnny, you sleepy little baby," she crooned in the voice she'd heard Kylie use with children. "We should go in and get you down for a nap."

She held out her arms to the baby and he allowed her to take him. She'd unclipped Bub's leash and the dog remained next to her.

Johnny snuggled close and he smelled of baby powder and lavender. "Oh, he doesn't smell bad today."

"They don't always smell bad," Max said. He picked up Linnie and Teddy in his arms. The two children giggled as he swung them around. "Do they?"

"Maybe not." She held Johnny close as they walked through the front door. Max led her to the kitchen.

"There's something in the slow cooker. Mom and Nonni went to Tulsa. Melody will be home later."

"It smells really good. What is it?" she asked.

"Nonni's roast. Meat, tomatoes, curry, parsnips, carrots and potatoes."

Sierra's mouth watered at the aromas seeping from the cooker. "Can they eat that?"

"As far as I know." He walked to the door to the dining room. "Dad, do you know what kids can eat?"

They heard a loud laugh from the stairs and a few minutes later Aldridge joined them in the kitchen. "Yeah, I think I can help you all out with that."

"The roast should be okay for them, shouldn't it?" Sierra asked.

"Oh, sure. For the older two, it's fine. It's been cooking all day, so it's nice and tender. Just cut it all up in small bites. You can mash up those vegetables for the little one." Aldridge tickled Johnny and the baby giggled. "Now, that is a fine little man. It was a shame about the accident. Patsy's husband was coming home from work and got hit by someone texting and driving. A real shame."

"It was a senseless tragedy," Sierra agreed. She held the boy out to Max's father. "Do you want to hold him?"

"No, I don't reckon I do. You look like you're doing just fine and I've got calves to feed. You all think you can manage?"

"Dad, you don't have calves to feed."

"Well, I have something to do." Faster than a jackrabbit, Aldridge was out the door.

"So, about feeding these children..." she said. "Let me see if Johnny will sit on the floor with his brother and sister, and we can fix their plates," Sierra offered.

She tried to put the baby on the floor but he clung to her and cried. Bub, worried by the commotion, nudged at the baby with his whiskery nose. Johnny stopped crying for a brief moment then started again.

"What do I do with him?" she asked Max.

"Hold him. I'm sure he'll stop crying soon."

"Maybe he likes cookies. Cookies always make me happy." Sierra found a cookie jar and grabbed a cookie for the baby and one for herself. "Do you think it's okay to give him this?"

"Of course it is." Max smiled at her as she offered the cookie to the baby. "You're doing just fine."

"Am I? Really? Because what if he has peanut allergies?"

"Don't worry so much. I've heard children are basically indestructible."

"I don't think that's the case." She looked down at the baby, who continued to cry. "Play some music. Babies like music."

He spoke to the speaker on the counter and music began to play. Sierra started to dance around the room with Johnny in her arms. He sobbed a few times but then his tears stopped.

As she moved around the kitchen with the baby, Max fixed plates and got the other two children seated at the table.

"You figured it out," Max said as he poured cups of milk for Teddy and Linnie.

"I can't do this all night." Already her right leg had begun to tighten. She paused for a moment to relax the muscles.

"Are you okay?" Max came up behind her and reached for Johnny. "I'll take a turn."

"We make a pretty good team." She gave him a look, imploring him to not comment, and he didn't. His attention had shifted to the children at the table. Sierra hurried over.

Linnie had her face down in her plate, licking carrots off the stoneware.

"Linnie, use the fork." She grabbed the small fork and helped the little girl to hold it.

Linnie looked at the fork, picked up a piece of meat with her fingers and plopped it into her mouth. She grinned and made happy noises. "Mmm."

"Is it good?" Sierra asked.

The little girl nodded and scooped more food into her mouth, chewing happily.

Teddy seemed more amenable to her help with the fork. Sierra scooped him up a bite and put it in his mouth. Bub waited nearby, hoping for scraps. Teddy obliged, dropping a parsnip on the floor. Bub sniffed and then sat back on his haunches. Not a fan of parsnips.

"No more of that, little man," Sierra scolded with a smile as she grabbed a napkin to clean up the floor.

She glanced up at Max, watching, Johnny in his arms. He swayed with the little boy, who now had his head on Max's shoulder, eyelids drooping as he dozed off.

"Do you want me to take him?" she whispered.

"Nope, but if you take the quilt off the back of the sofa and put it on the floor, he might sleep there for a bit."

"Will do." She hurried ahead of him to the living room and spread the quilt out.

Max knelt and settled the little boy, grabbing a pillow off the sofa and placing it against his back and then pulling part of the quilt up to cover him.

"You're a pro," Sierra whispered.

"I'm learning on the fly." He stood but then remained motionless as Johnny squirmed a bit before finding a comfortable spot and settling back to sleep.

"He didn't eat," Sierra said.

"I think he'll let us know if he's hungry." Max motioned her to the door. "What about you?"

"Starving. I didn't have time for lunch. We have a wedding this weekend and the entire thing seems so over the top. Today the caterer almost quit."

"But you brought them back on board."

"Yes, I did."

His hand went to her back as they walked to the kitchen. The touch took her by surprise but then she welcomed it. There was something about him, about his touch, that made her feel stronger.

And that made her want to run from his touch because she didn't want to be fooled, or let down. What if he wasn't the man she thought he was?

"Jack knew what he was doing when he put you in charge of the wedding venue," Max said as they entered the kitchen.

"I am the last person who should be planning other people's weddings. But I couldn't turn Jack down. I'm not sure where I would have been if he hadn't opened Mercy Ranch to us."

"No one understands more than Jack West." Max was quiet for a moment then asked, "Why do you consider yourself the last person who should be doing that job?"

She could give several answers to that question. She remembered her conversation with Jack, the one about dreams and finding what she loved. She didn't love weddings or planning weddings.

Max's hand moved from her back as if he had just realized that he still held it there, touching her in a way that seemed to protect.

She had never been guarded, cherished. Not by a father, a brother, a boyfriend. Solace and strength had come to her in waves, in knowing that God had protected her. Even when she'd felt alone, hurt, angry, God had known her pain, her sorrow.

Her heart ached, because she suddenly wanted to be the girl who believed in love, in beautiful weddings and everything that came with those dreams.

Max watched from the doorway as his mother and Sierra got the three children ready for bed. Sierra had been sitting with Linnie on her lap, reading the little girl a story. When Linnie would point to pictures, Sierra would give her answers. Occasionally, Linnie would repeat words. He'd been assured that the child did speak—she was just incredibly shy and had taken to wandering after her father's death.

Nonni appeared at his side, smiling up at him. "I want this house full of children, Maximus."

He bent to kiss the top of her head. "Don't worry, Nonni, Melody will give you grandchildren."

"Bah, I don't like that Andrew. He can't even be bothered to show up here and help plan the wedding. Too busy, he says." Then her eyes widened and she clasped a hand over her mouth. "Do not repeat that to your sister."

"I would never," he assured her. "Any reason why?"

"I don't know. I think I will never believe any man is good enough for our Melody."

"I think you're right about that. But I'm sure you also felt that way about my father when Mom first brought him to meet you."

His grandmother gave him a sheepish smile. "We always loved your father. He was a good man. A rancher. And he's still a good man. Andrew isn't your father."

He watched the scene in the living room, unsure of what to say to his grandmother. His mother had loved a cowboy and still did. Their story had the happy ending that Sierra found difficult to believe in. He hoped his sister would have the same.

"Have you heard from their mother?" Nonni asked.

"She'll be here soon. It seems a shame to put them to sleep only to have to wake them."

"Perhaps you could take them to their home and put them in their beds. She wouldn't have to pick them up here and take them back home."

"What a good idea. I should say something before they get them too settled."

Nonni's brows arched. "Maybe you should notice what is in front of your face?"

"What would that be?" he asked. "Sleepy children?"

"Oh, I think you know."

"Nonni, you should not hint, you're not good at it."

"I wasn't hinting," she told him as she patted his cheek. "I don't waste time hinting."

"I'm not sure what to say to that."

She gave him a pleased smile. "What can you say? I'm almost always right, so you should just agree."

"I think I should see about getting these children home."

"Yes, that's also a good idea. I'm glad I thought of it."

He gave her a sharp look that did nothing to quell her spirit. She laughed and patted his back.

Max walked over to Sierra and Linnie. "Nonni had an idea. She thinks we should take the children home and put them in their own beds so Patsy doesn't have to pick them up and take them home."

"That is a good idea." Sierra glanced at her watch. "But how do we get in?"

"She told me where I could find a spare key, in case we needed anything. I'll just call and let her know what we're up to."

He made the phone call, then they carried the children to Sierra's SUV and buckled them in. Bub got in the front seat with Sierra.

"I'll meet you there," she said as she closed her door.

He watched as she turned her car around and headed down the drive and then he got in his truck to follow.

It was just a short distance to the trailer park. But as Max rounded a curve in the road, he saw the orange glow of a fire.

Chapter Twelve

Sierra's heart caught in her throat at the sight of flames pouring from Patsy's trailer. There were no fire trucks at the scene yet but neighbors had gathered a safe distance away. She parked her car at the entrance to the trailer park.

People were shouting. Someone yelled that the fire department had been notified. Sierra got out of her car, giving the children in the back seat a cautious look. They were fortunately all sleeping. This was the last thing they needed to see.

"We can't do anything. It's a loss." Max's voice. His hand clasped her arm as if he feared she would run into the flames. "Come on, we need to make sure we stop Patsy."

She nodded. She glanced back at the trailer and thought about the Christmas tree, the gifts, the home that Patsy had built a life in.

"It shouldn't be like this," she said.

"I know." His arm was around her, comforting and warm as the December air sizzled and popped with the flames of the fire.

"What about their dog?"

"I'll check with the neighbors." He walked into the dark, the orange glow of the fire turning him into a wavering silhouette as he approached the group of people a short distance away. He disappeared from sight and she waited, praying he would be safe.

He returned a few minutes later smelling of smoke but he was safe and had Shep, leading him by a chain. The dog looked more than a little frightened.

"A neighbor unhooked him from his doghouse."

"I'm so thankful. I don't know what Linnie would do without Shep."

"Now that we have him, let's get the kids away from here."

"I can take them to Mercy Ranch. We have empty apartments."

"That's a good idea." Max opened her door for her. "You go and I'll wait for Patsy. I'll bring her there as soon as I can."

An explosion rocked the air, shaking the ground. The heat of the fire could be felt, even from a safe distance. Sierra froze, afraid to open her eyes, afraid the memories would trap her in the past. She could hear the children in the car, calling for their mother. Shep had jumped inside with them. A hand, warm and comforting, touched her arm.

"Sierra, listen to me. You're safe."

Slowly she opened her eyes and she looked up at him, sinking into his dark eyes, eyes that assured her that everything would be okay.

"I know I'm safe." Her voice shook as she said it, though. "I know I'm safe."

"Do you know that?" he asked.

She nodded. Taking a deep breath, she reached for his

hand and held it tight for a moment. "Yes. You have to call Patsy and let her know. And tell her not to worry."

He kissed her, taking her by surprise. Then she kissed him back because it felt safe in his arms.

"Go," he said. "I'll be there soon."

In the distance she could hear fire trucks. The lights, red and blue, flashed in the darkness. Sierra got in her car and shifted into Reverse. Bub moved as close to her as she'd allow. From the back seat, Shep gave a low growl.

"We're fine, Bub. We really are."

The drive to the ranch took ten minutes. Police cars and fire trucks zoomed past, heading to the trailer park. Sierra's phone rang. It was Kylie.

"Hey," Sierra answered.

"Carson just got a call. Patsy's trailer…"

"I know. We have the kids. She's been at the hospital with her mother and asked us to watch them. We were taking them home when we saw the flames."

"Poor Patsy. Where are you taking the kids?"

"To the ranch. I didn't know what else to do with them. It's almost Christmas. This isn't right or fair."

"We will make it right," Kylie said. "Can I bring anything?"

"I have no idea. I don't know what these little people need. I know that they don't like parsnips. Or carrots. They really like potatoes and homemade rolls. But I don't know what they need. At least we can give her a place to stay."

"Yes, we can do that." Kylie's tone was thoughtful. "Okay, I'm going to see what kinds of clothes we have around here and I'll be over shortly."

"Kylie, stay home with your family. There's nothing you can do tonight." Sierra surprised herself with those words. Weeks ago she would have wanted Kylie to take over. Especially if children were concerned.

"You're sure?" Kylie asked.

"I'm sure. We're fine for tonight. Tomorrow we'll start gathering up what they need."

She pulled up to her apartment, parking in the grass near the front door so she wouldn't have to carry the children quite so far. Bub was eager to get out, jumping and running around her as she got the door unlocked and then unbuckled the sleeping children.

A truck and car pulled up as she managed to get Linnie out of the back seat. The little girl slept soundly, which made her difficult to carry. Sierra brought her inside and down the hall to one of the downstairs apartments. When she returned to the main living area, Max was there with Teddy. The toddler had his pudgy arms around Max's neck.

"This one?" Max asked.

"Down here. We have a larger apartment that no one is staying in and it should work for them." She glanced toward the door, saw Patsy standing there with Johnny, looking lost and unsure. "Patsy, I'm so sorry."

Patsy face was pale, her eyes rimmed in red from crying. "We'll be okay. We've always been okay."

"Of course you will. But that doesn't make it easy." Sierra motioned her forward. "Follow me and we'll get you all settled."

Patsy followed her down the hall. Max had placed Teddy on the sofa in the one-bedroom suite. Linnie cuddled up to her brother, oblivious to their circumstances. Patsy stood in the center of the room with Johnny, holding him close, her eyes closed.

"Patsy, there's a playpen. I think Johnny could sleep in it. I'll go get it for you." Sierra showed the woman a chair. "Sit down and I'll be right back. And I'll get you some clothes."

"I'm fine. Really, I'm fine." Patsy smiled up at her. "I think I'm numb."

"That's understandable."

"Johnny can sleep with me tonight." Patsy stopped her from leaving. "Tomorrow we will figure something out."

"Are you sure?" Sierra asked.

"I'm sure. Clean clothes would be good, but I think I just want to sleep."

"Are you hungry? Thirsty?" Sierra asked as Max slipped from the room, leaving them alone.

"I'm good." Patsy sank down in the recliner and held her baby tight. "Tonight it all feels like a dream. Actually, a nightmare. Tomorrow it will be unfortunately all too real."

"I know," Sierra agreed. "Believe me, I know. And tomorrow, you'll have all of us. We'll be here to help you."

"Thank you." Patsy put a hand to her forehead. "Our dog. I didn't even think about Shep."

"He's here. I'll walk him and then bring him down here."

Patsy nodded. "Thank you. And tell Mr. St. James thank you."

Sierra stepped out of the apartment. She went to her own rooms, gathered up clothes and returned them to Patsy. Then she walked down the hall to the kitchen. She jumped when a tall form stepped from the shadows. But then she recognized the dark hair, the lean cheeks. He touched her arm.

"I didn't mean to scare you. I just wanted to make sure you're okay before I leave." Max held out a bottle of water. "And I thought you might need this."

"I do. Thank you." She unscrewed the top and took a long drink.

"Are you okay?"

"Yes, you just scared me. I didn't expect you to be there."

He gave her a long look that asked questions and, as difficult as it might be, she wanted to give him answers, a small window into her life. He'd become a friend and she wanted to give him the truth.

"I'm fine. Sometimes, in my head, I'm there again, in the cell, unable to escape."

"I'm a good listener if you want to talk." He took a seat at the kitchen island.

She closed her eyes, wishing she could do so without seeing the explosion, the helicopter, the prison cell, the men who had held her captive. She told him bits and pieces of a story she didn't really want to relive. He listened, his expression reflecting her pain.

Footsteps on the stairs alerted them to company. Glory appeared, looking a little wild with her curly hair going in all directions and her glasses missing from her pert nose. She probably couldn't see ten feet in front of her. She wouldn't see Max's shock or Sierra's eyes, glossy from unshed tears.

"Glory?" Sierra said. The younger woman blinked a few times.

"I heard people."

"We brought Patsy and her children here. Her home caught on fire tonight."

Glory blinked a few times. "Oh, no. Does she need anything?"

"Tomorrow. Go on back to bed."

"You're okay?" Glory asked.

"I am."

Glory gave Max a look and then nodded as if approving before she wandered back up the stairs.

"Are you sure you're okay?" Max asked.

In the recent past Sierra wouldn't have known how to answer that question. Tonight, though, she realized she really was okay. She wasn't unscathed, but she was whole.

"I am." She said it with a smile. "'I am more than a conqueror.'"

"Through Christ who strengthens you?" He paraphrased the verse.

He got up and made himself at home in her kitchen. He filled the teakettle with water and then opened the cabinets, looking for something.

"What are you doing?"

"Hot chocolate. My mother thinks it is the cure-all for everything."

"Do I appear to need curing?" Sierra asked.

Max gave her a careful look. "I don't think so, but it's been a long night and I want to do something for you."

"Thank you." She watched as he emptied a hot chocolate packet into a cup and then waited for the water to boil.

It took only a few minutes and he had a steaming cup of hot cocoa ready. He put it on the counter in front of her.

"Are you having one?"

He shook his head. "No, this is where I tell you goodbye. Because I know you need time and I know my presence doesn't help you."

"Your presence doesn't hurt me," she tried to reassure him. As she said it, she realized how much truth was in that statement. He made her feel calm. And safe.

"I somehow doubt that, Sierra. I want to make sure you're okay. But I don't want to be the reason for you to be upset."

"Is that what you think?"

He shrugged. "I'm not really sure."

"You don't upset me." She studied his face, his lean cheeks, his straight nose, the chocolate-brown curls. "I don't want you to think I'm afraid of you."

"I'm glad." He started to leave but stopped. "But I still think it's better if I leave. For both of us."

She was about to reach for him but changed her mind. In her present state she thought she might make mistakes. He seemed to be thinking more clearly and she had never felt less sure.

Max stood at the edge of the Cardinal Roost Trailer Park the next morning. The sun was barely over the horizon, the air was still cold and a breeze kicked up the smoldering ashes of the trailer that had been Patsy's home. Several others had joined him at the trailer, even though there was nothing any of them could do.

"This is a bad situation," Isaac said as he leaned against the side of his truck. "Everything Patsy owned. Everything she'd worked for. All of it gone."

"She's got her life and her children. If she hadn't been at the hospital with her mom…" Jack left the rest unsaid.

"Hopefully she'll see that as a blessing," Max said. "It's going to be hard to see any blessings when she's faced with this just weeks before Christmas, when she's been trying so hard to get her life together."

Jack sighed. "She's got a place at the ranch as long as she needs it. But there are other options. I've got something in mind."

"What's that?" Isaac asked.

"Remember the Cutter place that I bought a few months ago? Got it for a good price but it needs a lot of work. I wasn't planning on keeping it, I just didn't want it to fall down."

"That's the house in town, on Sunset Drive?" Max asked.

"That's the one. Not a big house but three bedrooms. Needs quite a bit of work."

"How do we get started on this?" Isaac asked.

"It needs a few new windows, some drywall, fresh paint, new appliances and some updates." Jack rubbed a hand across his chin. "You boys go have a look, tell me what you think. But let's keep this under our hats. I think if we're going to do something like this, we ought to make it the nicest Christmas gift Patsy has ever had. If we say too much, she might try to talk us out of it."

"We'll go see what we can do with it," Isaac told his father. "You in on this, St. James?"

Max nodded and headed for his truck. "I'm in on it. Meet you there."

"I have to drive my dad home first. I'll be there in a half hour."

Max drove the short distance to town and turned down the narrow street that had the wondrous name of Sunset. He guessed the street faced west. The houses were small but clean, the yards neat. The house Jack had bought sat the end of the street. The yard was a good size, the back fenced. A swing hung from an old oak tree.

The place had potential. In a normal situation, Max would guess it needed weeks, maybe months, of work. In this situation, with everyone pitching in, surely they could have it done by Christmas.

He got out of his truck and walked up to the house. It had good lines. The roof was straight. The house seemed to be structurally sound. A car pulled up behind his. Not Isaac.

Sierra. She smiled and headed his way. "Buying your-self a house?" she asked.

"Nope." He wasn't letting the secret out of the bag. "What are you doing out so early? And driving, not run-ning."

She whistled and Bub jumped from the car to join her.

"Bub asked me not to take too many runs like that. He didn't enjoy it. It made his feet sore for a couple of days."

"I can imagine." He walked up on the front porch of the house and studied the beams. It didn't surprise him that she hadn't answered the question about being out so early. "How's Patsy this morning?"

"I left them sleeping. I figured they didn't need to get up early today."

"That's probably good."

"About last night," she said. "Thank you. For the hot chocolate. For making sure I was okay. I know I send the wrong signals at times, but I'm working on that. I want you to know that I appreciated your kindness."

"I'm glad I could be there to show you that kindness, Sierra."

She slipped her hand into his. The gesture seemed odd at first, as if she wasn't comfortable with it. They walked off the porch and around the house.

"Do you think Patsy and the children could live here?" she asked.

"Well, I'm not really sure what to say to that."

"Oh, I see." She gave his hand a squeeze and let go. The dog pushed his way between them, as if making sure Max understood that there were boundaries.

"Do you?" he asked.

"Yes, it's a surprise, right?"

It was a surprise. The way she was a surprise. For him, at least. Maybe other people knew the little things about her. She was generous, funny, kind. He was discovering those things one layer at a time.

"I promised not to say anything," he admitted.

"It's okay, I have it figured out. We're having a get-together tomorrow at the apartment, but you're not invited," Sierra told him.

"Why is that and what are you doing?"

She gave him a secretive smile. "I can't tell. Not unless you tell."

"That isn't fair. But you can ask Jack and he'll probably tell you."

"Oh, I will ask him. If he's planning a Christmas surprise, I want to know."

"I'm sure you do."

"I do. I'm suddenly very Christmassy."

Sierra continued to walk next to him and he realized he liked her there, her fingers brushing against his. She also made him feel regret. Because he wouldn't be here long enough to get to know her better. Because he thought if they got too close, she would back away.

"We'll be working on the honeymoon blanket for Melody," she told him. "Also, they want to discuss the Christmas at the Ranch event. Pastor Stevens has a schedule and route for the church buses that will be picking people up."

"Do you have everything that you'll need?"

"The food is taken care of. We also have clothes and shoe donations, both new and gently used."

"This event is going to touch so many lives," he said as they came to the swing. He motioned for her to sit and she did.

He gave the swing a gentle push.

"This event has changed my life," Sierra said as the swing took her away from him.

"It wasn't exactly on my to-do list, either," he admitted. "But I'm glad they asked for my help."

"And now Jack has roped you into another project," Sierra told him. "This house."

"Do you think Patsy will like this?"

"I think she'll love it. And it has a fenced-in backyard for the children."

"That would ease Patsy's mind, I'm sure. Sierra, I…" Just then a truck pulled up in front of the house. Maybe it was better that he'd gotten interrupted. He'd been on the verge of asking her to have dinner with him. Not a meal with his parents, or something at the café. A real date. Just the two of them.

Definitely the wrong direction for his thoughts to be going. She didn't need to be another woman he left sitting, waiting for him to show up. Not that he could imagine ever forgetting her.

She glanced toward the drive where Isaac had parked and then at him. "Max?"

He shook his head. "Nothing. I need to get back to the ranch."

"Oh, okay." She looked confused and he thought that made sense. He was pretty confused, too.

That was a very good reason to walk away. He didn't want to go into this feeling confused or worried that he might be the next person to hurt her.

Chapter Thirteen

The women invited to Sierra's apartment Tuesday evening were not the quietest bunch.

Kylie and Melody had invited Rebecca West, Nonni, Doreena and Jack's housekeeper, Maria. Or perhaps she was his girlfriend. No one really questioned him in that regard. Patsy was also included, as was Holly from the café, Tish Stevens, the wife of Pastor Stevens, and several women that Sierra didn't know.

"Come and join us," Kylie told her after allowing her to pretend to make coffee for ten minutes.

"I'll be right there. I'm going to put the coffee in carafes and put out a few goodies for us to snack on."

She was making a tray of snacks when Melody joined her in the kitchen. Not for the first time Sierra noticed shadows under the younger woman's eyes.

"Do you need help with anything?" Melody asked as she entered the room.

"I'm good. I could ask the same of you." Sierra refilled the coffee maker with water and started a fresh pot.

"Me?" Melody asked.

"I work with a lot of brides and each one is different.

Each wedding is different. But they're all very happy. Are you happy about your upcoming wedding, Melody?"

Melody walked to the sink and looked out the window, keeping her back to Sierra. "To be honest, I just don't need all of this. I did it for Mom and Nonni."

"Then you need to tell them what you want. There can be compromises. Do what you love." Sierra caught herself by surprise. It echoed what Jack had encouraged her to do. She had spent a lifetime making choices based on what was the best way out, never on what she really, truly wanted.

"Do what I love?" Melody leaned against the counter to watch Sierra place cupcakes and cookies on the tray.

"Isn't it your wedding?" Sierra asked, looking up from the tray.

"You're only having this conversation with me because you dislike weddings," Melody teased.

"Maybe, but I don't dislike yours as much as some. You don't want two hundred white Christmas trees in the ceremony."

Melody laughed. "No, I don't."

"So?"

"Okay. Here's what I want. Two hundred fewer people, the ceremony at our church, a cake that you make, and pastries and appetizers made by Nonni. That's what I would pick, if it was up to me."

"Then let's do that," Sierra suggested.

"I think it's too late."

Sierra stepped forward and put her arm around the younger woman's shoulders. "It's never too late. Do what you want."

"And what is it that you want, Sierra?" Melody teased.

"A few less nosy friends," Sierra said as they walked

back to the living area where the women were working their needles through the pieces of fabric.

"The honeymoon quilt!" Melody exclaimed. "This is something I will always cherish. Not just the quilt, but the memories of making it."

With this group of strong females surrounding her, Sierra wondered if Melody had ever offered up one idea on her own wedding. But Melody was strong, too. She would survive this and she'd give her own ideas on her wedding. Even if it meant canceling the wedding at the Stable.

Everyone laughed as Kylie stepped into the circle to sew her patch onto the quilt. She poked her finger more than once and her seam had to be redone by Nonni. Sierra waited at the edge of the group. The laughter, the people who loved one another. This tradition should be a part of every wedding.

Nonni motioned her forward. "Come on, Sierra, your turn. Smile, smile, this is a good thing."

"I'm afraid I'll ruin it. I sew worse than Kylie."

Everyone laughed. Nonni pulled her forward. "I don't think that is possible."

"Oh, I guarantee it." Sierra took the piece of material and, with Nonni's help, sewed the square into place.

"Look at that. Very good. Straight, even seams. Look at Kylie's. Never accept her help in hemming your dress. Finish sewing your pieces of the quilt and then we will bring it all together."

Sierra sewed several more pieces of fabric together. For a minute she watched the other women as they laughed and carried on conversations about their homes, their lives and families. She didn't have anything to share. Bub nudged at her hand. She patted him but he nudged again.

"Time to go out?" she asked the dog. He stared up at

her with soulful eyes. "Of course it is. Let me grab the leash."

Kylie caught her eye as she snuck out with the dog. She gave a little wave and a nod. Sierra nodded back, thanking her. The evening was cold and she pulled on the jacket she'd grabbed on her way out.

As she slid her arms into the sleeves, the expensive evergreen, mountain scent of Max St. James closed in around her. How had his scent gotten so thoroughly into her jacket?

She walked to the barn. It was the last place she typically went, but Bub seemed intent on heading that way.

Bub took a trail that added twice the distance to the short walk. They walked through the front of the building into a different world, surrounded by the smell of hay and pine shavings and the sounds of horses shuffling in their stalls.

It was peaceful. She walked down the wide aisle between stalls. A small gray head peeked over one stall. She stopped to pet the animal.

"Ah-hh, how are you tonight, Buckshot?" She rubbed the horse's jaw and the animal nuzzled her sleeve. He was always the horse that asked for attention when she visited the stable. She pulled a piece of candy out of her pocket, unwrapped it and the horse lipped it off her hand.

Bub woofed in warning. He turned toward the closed doors she'd just come through.

Max stepped through the door.

"Bub, stay." The dog whined but he stayed.

"Were you going to sic your dog on me?" Max asked with a smile.

"I would never do that, but you should announce yourself before you sneak up on a person."

He walked a little farther into the building. "Sneak? I

opened a door and came in. What are you doing skulking around in here?"

"I needed some air. There are a lot of women in there," she said with a smile. "What are you doing here? Men don't sew the honeymoon quilt, do they?"

"No, but they drive the women back and forth from the sewing. My dad and I are visiting Jack. He sent me down here to look at your horse. I hope you aren't too attached?"

"To this old thing, never." She pushed a little at the horse, who shoved his nose at her.

"Never?" Max asked.

"Never. Why would you want him?"

"I'm going to lead him out of the stall," Max told her as he reached for a lead rope hanging on the wall.

"Okay, go ahead." She stepped back to watch. The horse, not the man. Although both were lean and athletic with just the right amount of muscle.

The horse was easier to trust. She kept him in his place, behind the door. They had an easy and uncomplicated friendship that she understood. Max was an unknown.

He led the horse out of the stall and walked him up and down the aisle of the stable. Next he cross-tied him in the center of the aisle and stepped back to give him a long look. Sierra stood next to him to look at the animal. A big horse with nice eyes. And yet this was the horse Isaac and the other men on the ranch used to prank their friends because he always bucked at the initial contact with a rider.

"Did they tell you he bucks?" she asked after several minutes of watching Max look the horse over and run his hands over the animal.

He glanced back at her as he raised the horse's legs to check its hooves. "Does he?"

"Did they ask if you want to ride him?"

"They might have," he answered.

"Hmm, they've never offered to sell him before."

Max gave the horse a pat on the neck as Sierra stepped forward to pet the animal. She ran a hand down his neck and he leaned in.

"He seems to like you."

"We're friends. I come out and visit him from time to time."

Max moved around the horse. "Have you ever ridden him?"

"Are you kidding? I don't want to get thrown."

"I have a feeling he wouldn't throw you."

She arched a brow. "I'm not a horse person and I've been told a horse can sense that."

"He also knows you like him. I bet you even bring him treats."

"I don't like him," she insisted. The horse made a liar of her and nuzzled her pocket.

He gave her a knowing look that was far too cute, his dark curls in disarray. "Yeah, you do."

"I have to go. I have…stuff to do."

She spun on her heels to leave and she could hear his laughter chasing after her. No way would she join her laughter with his. She was making a grand exit. Or so she told herself. If she was being honest, she was running scared.

But isn't that what she always did when life got complicated?

Max studied the horse a bit longer, knowing he wouldn't buy the animal. Not for himself. Maybe for Sierra. Maybe she needed this horse to truly belong here. To him, it seemed as if she wasn't putting down roots in Hope. She was just biding her time and trying to figure out what came next for her.

She attended church but, until recently, she hadn't been too involved. She didn't socialize much. She had avoided pets and friendships. She didn't date.

If she had roots, things that made her feel as if this was her home and not just the place she was staying, he thought it might take some of the shadows from her eyes. He looked at the horse again.

"Is that how you feel?"

The horse nudged at him. Max brushed a hand down the sleek gray neck and led the animal back to his stall. "I understand. I like her, too."

"Talking to yourself?"

Max jumped and saw Isaac waving at him. "Did you want to ride him?"

"Nope. I was told you all like to play this joke on people from time to time."

Isaac grinned. "Now, who told you that? Sierra?"

"She was down here petting him," Max told him. "I think she's kind of attached to him. Why don't you give him to her?"

"That wouldn't be nearly as interesting as selling you this horse and letting you give him to her. Nah, I don't think I'll give her this horse." Isaac chewed on a piece of straw and stared at the horse then at Max. "Good thing I'm deaf in the left ear or I would have thought you said you like her."

"Good thing you can't hear," Max said. He latched the stall door and hung the lead back on the hook. The horse's head came over the stall, lipping at Max's jacket.

"He wants this." Isaac stepped forward with a chunk of carrot. "He likes treats. He doesn't like men."

"I'll buy him," Max said. "If he's really for sale."

"He wasn't for sale and still isn't. I do have some ethics. The people on this ranch are family. That makes Sierra kind of like a sister to me."

"And what do you think I would do to Sierra?"

"Hurt her."

Max shoved his hands in his jacket pocket. "Isaac, I haven't wanted to hit someone in a long time. As a matter of fact, you were the last person I wanted to hit. I guess it makes sense that you'd be the person pushing me to do it again."

"You know you don't have the best track record on dating. What was it you told me? More than one woman has been forgotten because you get busy working and leave them sitting at home alone. That isn't the most gentlemanly thing to do."

"I agree. Which is why I haven't been doing any dating lately. A woman has to mean more than business."

"That sounds like a good philosophy. But does Sierra mean more to you than business? Or is she just a girl from Hope, and pretty soon you'll be going back to wherever you've been living with your big cars and fancy helicopters?"

A shout from outside the barn stopped the conversation. "What was that?" Max asked.

Isaac gave him a look and pointed to his ear.

"Sorry, I heard something. It sounded like Sierra." He headed for the barn door. Isaac fell in next to him.

When they got outside they saw Sierra standing in the middle of the yard in a panic.

"What's wrong?" he asked as they drew closer. The

women from the quilting session were pouring out of the apartment.

"I can't find Bub. He took off as we were walking back to the apartment." Sierra kept her gaze trained on the horizon.

"I'm sure he didn't go far," Max said encouragingly. "We'll find him."

"What if he doesn't come back?" A lone tear streaked down Sierra's cheek. "This is silly. He's just a dog. They run off. They chase things. They come back."

"He's around here somewhere. Call him again," Isaac said.

She whistled and called the dog. Nothing. Bub had been trained to be a companion dog. He knew to stay by her side or to come to her the minute she needed him. The dog wouldn't willingly ignore her.

"What's wrong?" Max's mom, Doreena, was the first of the women to reach them. She took one look at Sierra and folded her in her arms. Why hadn't he thought to do that?

"The stupid dog," Sierra said. "I didn't want a dog. I don't even like animals."

Of course she didn't. She didn't like the dog. Or the horse in the barn. She pretended she didn't like children. The truth of the matter was, she loved deeply but didn't want to be hurt by loss.

"Let's go look for him," Max offered. "We can check the roads, Isaac can check the fields."

His mother released Sierra from her embrace. "Yes, go with Max. I'm sure Bub is just chasing rabbits. Dogs do that."

Sierra wiped a finger under her eyes.

Max motioned her toward his truck.

They drove down to the main road. Max scanned the

roadside and knew she was doing the same. They both wanted to see the dog trotting in the ditch, heading home.

"I can't believe I'm acting like this. I didn't even want a dog." She had her window down, allowing the cold air to blow in.

"You're acting like this because you love the dog." Max slowed to check ditches as they drove.

"Yes," she admitted. "I love Bub."

They found him a few hundred feet down the road, sitting dazed and unmoving.

Together they approached the dog. He'd obviously been hit. When he saw Sierra, he gave a low bark, then whimpered and settled on the ground. She sank to her knees next to him. Max pulled out his phone and called Isaac so he could let everyone know they'd be heading to the veterinarian.

"Let's get him in the truck," Max told her, resting a hand on her shoulder.

"Yes, of course." Sierra put her arms around the dog and struggled to her feet.

"Sierra, I can carry him for you."

"I know." She stubbornly headed for the truck, her face buried in the dog's neck.

"Okay, you can carry him." He followed her, opening the back door so she could slide the dog in. Instead she got in with him.

"Do you think he'll be okay?" she asked as they made the short drive to the local vet.

"I think he will be. I can't believe whoever hit him didn't stop." Max glanced in his rearview mirror. "Are you okay?"

"I'm good. We're good. Aren't we, Bub?"

They pulled up to the veterinarian's office. A truck

pulled in right after. Doc Erikson was close to retirement and dealt more with farm animals than pets.

"Doc," Max said as he hopped out of the truck, "thanks for meeting us."

Max lifted the dog from the truck and carried him to the building, Sierra at his side like a worried mother hen.

"Bring him on into the exam room." Doc flipped on light switches as they went.

Max placed Bub gently on the table. The dog whimpered as Doc Erikson did a quick exam.

"I don't think it's anything serious. I'm going to do an X-ray, so the two of you go on out. I'll call you back in when I'm done. He's a nice-looking dog, Sierra. That's your name, isn't it?"

"Yes, Sierra."

Max led her back to the waiting room and they stood looking at dog food and grooming brushes rather than taking a seat in one of the hard plastic chairs that had been there for as long as Max could remember.

"You think I'm ridiculous, don't you?" Sierra asked as she fiddled with the canned dog food, straightening the stacks.

"Nope."

"Broken beyond repair?" she asked with only a hint of humor.

"I think you've had some hard knocks and that you've survived. You're still surviving."

"I had a dog once, for two days." She cleared her throat. "Until my dad got mad at my mom and decided the best way to pay her back was to hurt me. He grabbed that dog and told my mom she would never make another decision without asking him first. I never saw the dog again. From the outside looking in, my parents were educated, decent people. My dad was an accountant for a company in Cleveland. My mom managed several clothing stores. We had a beautiful home in a good neighborhood—" Abruptly she stopped talking as if surprised she'd said so much.

"I'm sorry."

"It's okay. I survived." She paced the room then she returned to his side.

He opened his arms and she stepped into his embrace. Her head rested on his shoulder and he couldn't remember ever feeling like that, as if someone belonged in his arms, in his life. His hands were on her back and he couldn't remember a time that he'd ever felt more like he'd come home than at that moment with Sierra in his arms, trusting him.

The door to the exam room opened. She stepped back, gave him a shy smile and faced Doc with a hopeful look.

"He's pretty banged up, bruised and sore. He has a broken bone in his front leg that I'm going to set. In a couple of weeks, he'll be as good as new."

Sierra rushed to Doc and gave him a tight hug. "Thank you."

The vet laughed and patted her shoulder. "You're welcome. I hope the two of you have a long and happy relationship."

"Oh, we're not dating," she said.

Doc chuckled. "I meant you and the dog. But okay."

Sierra's face turned a shade of red Max hadn't seen very often, and she raised a hand to cover her embarrassment.

"Now, don't you worry about a thing. You can probably trust Max to stay close without a leash, too." Doc called out to them as they headed for the truck.

Max drove Sierra back to her apartment on Mercy

Ranch. The place was quiet, most of the lights were off. Kylie met them at the door, a finger to her lips.

"Patsy and the kids just went to bed," she said as she opened the door for them. "How is he?"

"Broken leg," Sierra answered. "I don't know what I would have done… Not that I'm attached or anything."

Max shot her a look as he settled Bub on his bed in the living room.

Kylie gave her an equally dubious look. "No, of course you're not attached."

Sierra sat next to the dog on the floor. "Okay, I'm attached. And I hold you responsible." She pointed a finger at her friend.

Kylie smiled. "I'm glad I could help. I'm out of here. Carson and the kids are at Jack's, waiting to drive me home."

Sierra got to her feet and walked her friend to the door. Max guessed that was his cue to go. It was late. As he made to depart, Sierra closed the door. She turned to face him.

"I should go," he said.

"I could make tea," she offered.

"As tempting as that is…" he said. But it wasn't tea that tempted him.

He could very easily promise her things. The thought left him shaking in his muddy old boots even as he took a step toward her.

"I'm thirsty."

The tiny voice from the hall stopped him cold. They both pivoted in the direction of the child who appeared, standing just feet away from them.

"I'll get you a drink and then it's back to bed," Sierra said as she took Linnie by the hand. Shrugging, she gave him an apologetic look.

Max settled for kissing her cheek. "I'll check on you tomorrow."

Sierra didn't object. It was better that way. He didn't know how she felt, but he knew that each moment he spent with her made it that much more difficult for him to leave at the end of the month.

Chapter Fourteen

"How's your dog?" Melody asked when she showed up at the Stable chapel on Saturday following the quilting of the honeymoon blanket. They had just over a week to pull off the Christmas at the Ranch event, and the committee members were supposed to meet. That meant Max. Sierra hadn't seen much of him since the night Bub had gotten hit.

"He's much better. He's at home with Patsy and the children."

Sierra pulled out a notebook. "Melody, I made a few plans. For a small, more intimate wedding. For you."

Melody took the notebook and looked it over. "Oh, Sierra, this is beautiful. But my family…"

"Would want you to be happy. They're planning this wedding because they think it's what you always wanted, and they want you to be happy." Sierra smiled at the younger woman. "And you're planning a wedding to make them happy."

"I never thought about it like that," Melody said in a tone that became quiet, thoughtful. "I just don't know."

"Is this about the ceremony?" Sierra asked. "Or are you more worried about the marriage?"

Silence hung between them as Melody studied the notebook Sierra had given her to look at, avoiding eye contact. "Andrew cheated on me. To be honest, I don't even know if he wants this wedding. We talk on the phone but I haven't seen him in over a month."

"Oh, Melody." Sierra didn't know what else to say.

"I shouldn't have told you. I mean, he apologized and said it won't happen again."

"Do you really believe that?" Sierra regretted the harshness of her words. "I'm sorry, it isn't my place to judge. I just know that when a husband or father cheats, he's cheating on more than his wife. He's breaking a promise."

"I worry that I'm not judging Andrew fairly because I want him to be more like my father. He's Andrew. I have to accept that."

"Yes, we have to accept people for who they are. But you have to like who he is. At least most of the time."

"Yes, you're right. And I do like him." Melody looked a little startled. "I mean love. I love him."

"Do you trust him?"

Melody stared up at the ceiling. "That's a good question."

"It's a question I would want to be able to answer before I married someone."

Melody looked down at the notebook in her hands. "I wanted a crazy, extravagant wedding when I was a kid, but now I just want simple. I want to stand at the front of the church in front of people I care about with the man I care about."

"That sounds pretty perfect to me. And you can do that in a big venue or church. If it is special to you, that's all that matters."

"Right," Melody said. "I know you have donations

rolling in for the Christmas event, but someone said you're also gathering up donations for Patsy and her children."

Sierra allowed the younger woman to change the subject. "Yes, they have the clothes on their backs, shoes, a few toys each. But they're going to need so much more as they get settled in a new home."

"A tree with gifts, decorations, dishes, food, toys and clothes."

"It's a lot," Sierra admitted. "As for Christmas decorations, I have enough for the Christmas event and for Patsy. The Jones/Gunner wedding was an overdecorated mess. The bride had to push her way through the forest like Gretel trying to get to Hansel. I'm sure they love each other and they'll have a beautiful marriage, but..."

"God bless them," Melody murmured.

They both laughed.

"Yes. And they left behind some of those trees and decorations. We have plenty to decorate Patsy's new home and present it to her as a Christmas gift."

"Perfect." Melody jumped up. "Let's drive to town, do some shopping and go by the house."

The invitation took Sierra by surprise and, normally, she would have declined. Today, however, she found herself at loose ends and wanting to spend time with a friend. A friend who happened to be Max's sister.

A few minutes later, they were parking in front of Rebecca's salon and day spa. Christmas music played from a speaker attached to the underside of the awning. There were people walking along the sidewalks, going in and out of shops. The growth of the town, thanks to Jack West's time and investment, had changed so many lives.

"It's very festive, isn't it?" Melody observed as they

walked along the sidewalk. "I do love my hometown. Even when we lived in Tulsa, this was always my town."

"I think it's the closest thing I've ever had to a hometown." Sierra stepped aside for a young couple to pass by. "I hadn't planned on staying. I still wonder sometimes if I should move on. After all, Jack didn't start Mercy Ranch for people to live here permanently. It's a place to start over, to get physically and emotionally ready to get back to life."

"I think Jack would let you stay forever. You're one of his kids."

Sierra smiled at the statement. "Yes, maybe."

"Let's get a cupcake." Melody grabbed her hand and pulled her toward the bakery. "I know they're not as good as yours, but we can sit down, have coffee and something full of calories."

"I'm not against other people's cupcakes," Sierra said. Then she noticed the sign on the window. Cupcake Café For Sale By Owner.

"Oh, no!" Melody exclaimed as they walked through the door. "I love this place."

The small establishment was packed, with only a few tables available. Melody and Sierra made their way to the front to peruse the glass case of cupcakes. The owner, a woman named Millie, appeared from the back to help them.

"Millie, why are you selling?" Melody asked without preamble.

"I thought I could live here, away from my grandchildren. It was our dream to have a lake home. But Fred and I miss our kids."

Melody gave Sierra a pointed look that Sierra ignored.

"We'll be sorry to see you go," Sierra told the woman.

Millie brightened. "You're a baker, Sierra. Would you

want to buy it? We don't want to compete with Holly, but during the summer we were going to expand our menu to items she doesn't offer. Fancy little sandwiches, herbal teas."

"Oh, I don't think so. I have the Stable to run."

"But—" Melody started.

Sierra cut her off. "But I would love a French vanilla cupcake and a bottle of water."

Melody rolled her eyes. "I'll have the same. And coffee for me."

They found an empty table in the corner and sat down. "Sierra, this place looks like it was made for you. You love to bake. You love tea."

"Yes, I do like to bake. But I like to bake in the comfort of my own home." Sierra took a bite of the vanilla cupcake and closed her eyes. "This is amazing."

Find your dream, Jack West had told her. Could her dream really be a cupcake bakery in Hope? She tried to picture herself here, baking, greeting customers.

The door of the café opened and Max walked in. He saw them and headed their way.

"Hey, big brother, imagine seeing you here." Melody stood to give him a hug.

Max removed his cowboy hat and grabbed a chair from an empty table to join them. "What are the two of you up to?"

"We just wanted to get out. It's close to Christmas and I think Sierra spends all of her time at the ranch. Hope at Christmas is the best, so here we are."

"Here you are," he repeated. His gaze connected with Sierra's and she felt it her cheeks heat up. "I saw your car and thought you might be in here. You should come by the house on Sunset. I think we're going to have it done for Christmas."

"We were just discussing how we could decorate it for them." Sierra explained the idea and Max agreed.

"Perfect. Stop by and see how things are going after you finish shopping."

Sierra started to object but Melody told him that they'd be by as soon as they finished shopping.

Max and Pete, one of the Mercy Ranch residents, finished the section of wall they'd been drywalling and Max grabbed the bottle of water he'd left in the windowsill. A truck pulled up outside. He watched as his sister and Sierra got out. The two of them stood in the yard of the little house Jack West was having remodeled for Patsy.

Max moved on to the next room. They had men working on replacing lights and faucets. Someone else was painting kitchen cabinets. They didn't all work at the same time but it was a well-orchestrated project. It had been keeping him busy and keeping his mind off the tangled-up situation with Sierra.

Sierra walked in and glanced around the brightly lit room and nodded. Then her gaze collided with his. Her hazel eyes warmed and her mouth turned a bit in a smile that appeared to be just for him. His mouth went a little dry.

"You guys are amazing," Melody said in her most enthusiastic tone. She smiled at Isaac and Joe. The two were putting Sheetrock on the wall between the living room and the dining room.

"We're here to help," Sierra told him. "We can paint, clean…whatever you need us to do."

Isaac stepped forward, obviously glad for extra hands. "If you'd like to put liners in the drawers and bottom of the cabinets, you can."

"Girl stuff," Melody said in a false whisper to Sierra.

"Do you know how to do drywall, sis?" Max asked.

"Well, no, but I can learn anything I set my mind to."

He shook his head. "Not this time. I'd hate for you to get hurt when your wedding is just two months away. Speaking of, when is Andrew coming up to see you again?"

Her face crumpled just a bit and he had to wonder what he'd said wrong.

"It might be after Christmas," she finally answered. "He's taking his parents on a cruise for Christmas."

"Oh." He tried his best to come up with an answer that didn't make it sound like he wanted to hunt the guy down. "I suppose that makes sense because next year he'll be a married man at Christmas."

"Right," Melody said with a smile that didn't reach her eyes.

His gaze shot past her to Sierra and he saw that her expression showed the same disbelief he felt. And that didn't bode well for the Valentine's wedding.

"How's Bub doing?" he asked Sierra as the men started moving their tools to the next room.

"He's better. Hobbling around, but not quite ready to keep up with me. He's with Patsy and her children."

Melody made a big show of pulling her phone from her purse. Max watched, wondering what she might be up to. She'd never been good at subterfuge. She'd been the kid who would be holding cookies in her hand while denying that she stole cookies from the kitchen.

"Oh, wow, I completely forgot," she said with a dramatic flourish.

"What's that?" Max asked, as if he really thought she had something she'd forgotten.

"I have a thing, an appointment. Not really an appointment. Mom wants me to do something for her. Christmas stuff. Sierra and I rode together."

"Oh, I can leave anytime," Sierra offered.

"I know you want to stay and help. I'd hate for you to have to leave because of my forgetfulness." Melody's gaze connected with his.

Max nearly shook his head at his sister but decided to play along. "I don't mind giving you a ride home, Sierra."

"Are you sure?" Melody asked. "I know you're busy here."

"I was going to head out in an hour or so," Max assured her.

"Sierra, do you mind?"

"No, of course not. If Max doesn't mind, that is."

Melody gave Max a quick hug then Sierra. "Wonderful. Thank you for being so understanding. And I'll see you at church tomorrow."

"Oh." Sierra hesitated. "Yes, of course."

And out the door she went.

"You realize she set you up?" Max asked.

Sierra smiled, her eyes brightening. "I kind of got that vibe. But I've been wanting to help out, so here I am. Put me to work."

"We've got a room or two that we really can start painting."

"Let's do it."

He gave her a quick once-over. "You're going to want something else to wear. I think I have a work shirt in my truck. I'll be right back."

She followed him to the front porch and he returned with the shirt. He held it out and she put it on. She buttoned it up the front. Standing close, he caught a whiff of her wildflower-and-sunshine perfume and thought about that scent lingering on his shirt.

Fifteen minutes later, they were in what would probably be a child's bedroom. Maybe it would be Linnie's. For that reason, he'd grabbed a can of paint that was labeled "Pink Shell."

"What do you think?" he asked Sierra. "Will this make a good color for a little girl's room?"

"It's the perfect color."

He handed her a roller and opened the paint can, stirring it with the stick he'd found in the box of supplies.

Plastic sheets had been laid down on the floor. The window trim had been removed, so they didn't have to worry about taping it off. They poured paint into two trays and went to work. She started on one wall, he on the other.

"Nice color." Isaac stepped into the room and made an approving face as he nodded. "I'm guessing this will be the little girl's room? Rebecca ordered bedding and someone donated a pretty twin bed and dresser for her."

"Do we know which room the boys will share?" Sierra asked.

"The room next to the bathroom is a little bigger than this one and has two closets. The largest bedroom will be Patsy's." Isaac gave them the rundown. "It's going to make a good little house for raising her kids."

"It's an amazing thing for your dad to do," Sierra added.

Isaac shrugged. "Other people are pitching in. It's a community effort, just like Christmas at the Ranch. You know my dad, he doesn't want the credit. He said he was just fortunate to get this place cheap. I'm going to skate out of here now. You two lock up when you're finished painting."

"Will do," Max assured him. He liked Isaac, on most

days. But he noticed too much. His shrewd gaze locked with Max's as he headed for the door.

If Sierra noticed, she didn't make mention of it. She quietly went back to work on the last wall. He joined her and they finished it quickly. They could now paint the area they'd avoided, the top of the wall to the ceiling. Max pulled out the special brush for the edging.

Sierra put the roller down on the pan he'd brought in and stretched. He tried to pretend he wasn't at all moved by this moment. He kept picturing the two of them in a home, painting a room pale pink for a…

He blinked at the thought. Nope. He was not going there.

She stepped next to him, watching as he did the trim work. He kept painting, trying hard to tamp down all thoughts of domesticity. Did she even want children?

As he finished, she took a step back, positioning herself so that she could look out the window that had a view of farmland. He finally put his brush down and stretched to relieve the knots in his shoulders. He moved to her side, wondering at her stillness.

"Hi," she said in a soft voice, as if her thoughts were somewhere other than this room with him.

He caught a wispy strand of her hair and let it slide between his fingers. "I don't want to scare you."

"Sometimes you do." She leaned her cheek against his shoulder. "Not for the reasons you think, though."

"No?"

She shook her head. "You frighten me because I don't want to be hurt. I don't want to miss you when you leave. And I will. That scares me. That makes me want to walk away and hopefully you'll walk in the other direction and we'll just go on with our lives and it won't hurt."

Why had he avoided relationships? He briefly remembered that he wasn't someone who could be counted on. At least not the way she needed.

But he wanted to be that person. For her.

"I want to kiss you." He pushed the strand of hair behind her ear. "I want to know that it's what you want, too."

"It's what I want." She touched his cheek with her fingertips and her hazel eyes softened. "I want you to kiss me more than I want you to walk away."

He touched his lips to hers, wondering how he'd gone from a guy who couldn't remember a date to a man who wouldn't ever forget this woman.

Chapter Fifteen

He drove Sierra home, neither one of them in the mood for chatter. When they got back to the ranch, she jumped out of his truck and hurried up the sidewalk, not waiting for Max to follow. But he did. She glanced back, smiling at him as he took quick steps to catch up. He had a feeling he might follow her anywhere.

Once, when he was about seventeen, his dad had told him it would happen like this. "Son," Aldridge had said, "you don't have to chase after love. One of these days it will happen and it will be unexpected, sneaking up on you when you aren't looking for it." He'd asked his dad how he would know it was love. His father had told him, "You'll know it's love because you will follow that girl anywhere."

"You could at least wait for a guy to stop the truck," he called out after her.

"It was stopped." She laughed breathlessly.

"Barely," he said as he caught up with her. "And you're beautiful when you laugh."

She stopped laughing and turned to stare up at him, as if she hadn't felt what he'd been feeling all this time.

But she had. He could see it in her expression, in the soft look in her eyes.

"I suddenly can't breathe," she said.

"Don't stop breathing. That would be awkward."

"I don't know what to say right now."

"Say you think I'm beautiful, too?" he teased.

Her laughter returned. "No one needs to tell you that. I think your mom and Nonni probably told you that too much when you were a little boy and look how you turned out."

"Sierra…" he began.

She shook her head. "No, don't say anything."

"There's a spider crawling up your arm."

"Stop."

"No, for real." He swiped it off and she shuddered and brushed at her arms.

"I hate spiders." She shuddered again. "Really, really hate them."

"I'm sorry, I should have just brushed it off."

"Yes, next time do that. Don't say anything at all, just get rid of it. Because eww, spiders."

She shuddered again and wiped her hands down her arms. He smiled a little, but not enough for her to see. He reached for her hand to stop her from walking away. He didn't know what he planned to say to her but the expression on her face warned him to tread carefully.

They were in unknown territory, he realized that. They were both feeling their way through the dark, unsure of what they were experiencing. He wanted to tell her it was the most real thing he'd ever felt. More than owning his first company, more than buying back the ranch for his parents.

This mattered in a way nothing ever had. He pulled her close and kissed her, because words would just ruin everything. What if he laid his heart out and she didn't feel what he felt?

She kissed him back, pulling away slowly to whisper his name, tears shimmering in her eyes. "I'm so confused by you."

"That isn't what I want." He opened the door for her.

Bub must have known they were home. He was already at the door, waiting for her, casted leg and all.

"I'm going to go now," Max said.

She nodded, her hand sliding down his arm. "Oh, your shirt."

Shrugging out of it, she handed it to him before he walked away.

There were men down by the barn, so rather than head home, he walked that direction. Joe, a longtime resident of the ranch, waved. Joe was an amputee but with his one good arm he managed to keep things running at Mercy Ranch. He'd told Max that when he'd arrived at the ranch, he'd just about given up on his life. He'd been a medic in the army and had planned on going to medical school but an explosion had changed everything for him. Now he was a ranch foreman, and a good one. But he was also going to school to be a psychologist because he said he could still help people heal, just in a different way.

"What brings you to Mercy Ranch on a sunny Saturday? Or is that a silly question?" Joe asked, walking to the fence to meet Max.

"I have a question," Max said.

"Shoot," Joe said. He leaned on the fence and, after a quick look back at the men who were working steers into a round pen, he gave Max his full attention.

"Does Sierra ride or does she just pet that gray bucking horse you all use to trick people?"

Joe laughed at that. "Buckshot?"

"Is that his name?"

"It is. And I guess she will ride from time to time but I didn't know she had an affinity for that horse. They bought him at auction. He was a rodeo horse and had recently thrown two or three unsuspecting owners."

"So you keep him around for fun to prank people?"

Joe grinned. "Yep. And we're not too ashamed of that. We only put a good rider on him, someone we know can handle it. I think Carson rode the daylights out of him when we put him on Buckshot."

"Yeah, I would reckon Carson would. Too bad Colt hasn't come back to Hope." Max hadn't thought of Colt West in years. Colt was the younger brother of Carson West. Jack's children had been gone for years, left with his wife when she'd finally tired of living with a drunk.

Jack had since gotten sober and turned his life around, but it looked as if Carson and Isaac might be the only ones in the forgiving mood. Colt and Daisy, their sister, were still living lives far from Hope.

"Yeah, well, I don't know Colt other than what I've seen on TV. He's a good bullfighter and used to ride some mean bulls, but I don't know how he is with horses. Buckshot, though, he isn't going to settle down anytime soon. We're guessing he's about ten, so he's spent a big part of his life bucking for a living."

"Would Isaac really sell him?" Max asked.

Joe shrugged and gave Max a shrewd, narrow-eyed look. "Why would you want that horse? I just told you, he isn't much of a saddle animal."

"I don't want him for myself."

Joe gave a slow nod and his eyes narrowed a bit more. "Who are you thinking might want that horse and what's the difference in owning it and being able to pet it from time to time?"

Because Sierra had lost too much in her life and she was afraid to get attached. Those words ran through his mind but they weren't something he could say to this man, basically a stranger.

"I want to give him to Sierra," he finally admitted. "She's attached to that horse and I don't want him sold. I don't want her to come out here one day and see the horse is gone. If I buy him, he's hers for good or until she's tired of him."

"She can't ride him," Joe emphasized, as if Max didn't know.

"I don't think riding him is important to her. There's probably two dozen horses on this ranch she can ride."

"I reckon that's the truth, but I also reckon if you buy this horse for her, you're making a statement."

"Regardless, I want this horse for Sierra."

"I'll let Isaac know."

"Thanks, Joe."

He walked away half pleased with himself and half afraid of what Joe had said about the horse making a statement. Sierra needed to know that this horse she was attached to wasn't going anywhere. Sometimes animals stayed, people stayed.

He pushed those thoughts to the back of his mind because he wasn't sure how he could stay in Hope.

But he also wasn't sure how he could leave.

Sunday after church Sierra joined Kylie, Melody, Nonni and Doreena along with several other women from the church. They had bags and boxes of items for the Christmas at the Ranch celebration.

Sierra backed her SUV up to the porch of the Stable and got out. There were a half dozen other vehicles waiting to do the same. The community had outdone itself in supporting the event that would make Christmas a lot merrier for everyone in and around Hope.

"Where are we going to put all of this?" Kylie asked as she came around the side of the car.

"Good question!" Sierra looked in at the boxes loaded in the back of her SUV. "I already have one storage room almost full. I think this can go in my office. I've got tables set up in the reception arena. I have a clothing section, toys, household goods, parent gifts. We'll need one to two people to oversee each section when the event happens next Saturday. We will also have the kitchen staff and food. So we'll need tables for the meal."

"Wow." Kylie blinked a few times. "Where have you been hiding this person?"

Sierra teasingly punched her friend's arm. "I haven't hidden her."

"No, seriously, something has changed," Kylie said.

"Nothing has changed. God and I have had a long talk. Lately, He's helped me find peace. It's the chapel."

"The wedding chapel?"

Sierra motioned for Kylie to follow her. "It's best in the morning but afternoon is also spectacular. It's the windows."

Kylie looked extremely puzzled. "Okay, show me because I'm obviously not getting it."

Sierra led Kylie through the front lobby of the Stable to the chapel. Sunlight streamed through the stained-glass windows, bathing the large chapel with its pine walls and vaulted ceilings in golden sunlight. The room smelled of pine, flowers, evergreen and sunshine.

"This room. I spend so much time in here. Everyone believes I'm always down here planning the next wedding, but sometimes I'm here because in this room I feel His presence here." Sierra sighed. "This room is where

I've found more emotional healing and peace than anywhere else. Ever."

Kylie's eyes turned liquid and she hugged Sierra.

"Don't push it," Sierra said with a smile because, really, she no longer meant it.

Kylie wiped at her eyes. "Never. I can't put into words how happy I am for you, Sierra. We've been friends for several years and we've walked through some dark times together."

"And we've found the light together."

"Yes, the Light."

Sierra looked around the chapel and sighed again. "I do love this place. I think for a time it was just the place where I chose to be because I didn't know where else to be. Jack pushed me and I resented it, but this job has helped me to figure some things out. It is also helping me to plan the next phase of my life."

"This sounds serious," Kylie said as the two of them stood looking at the amber stained-glass windows.

"Jack told me to find my dream, what makes me happy. Yesterday I called and spoke to Millie at the Cupcake Café. I'm thinking about buying it. I don't want to leave Hope. This is my home. But I'm ready to start a real life here, not an existence."

"I'm so happy for you, Sierra," Kylie said.

"I'm happy, too," Sierra said. "Happy but afraid. In the back of my mind, I'm waiting for the other shoe to drop."

"Life isn't perfect. There will be ups and downs." Kylie shrugged. "But you get back up and keep moving forward."

"Thank you."

They made their way back outside. Melody had an armload and she gave them a curious look but didn't ask questions.

"Where do we take it all?" Melody asked.

"If we're going to set up the reception arena, let's go ahead and haul things in there." Sierra thought of something else. "I didn't think about feeding everyone today."

Kylie grinned. "Don't worry, I did. The men are on their way with food. They're going to fire up the grills and start cooking for all of the workers."

Sierra grabbed a box and headed for the reception arena. "Let's get this party started," she quipped over her shoulder.

"Did I hear party?" Nonni called out, doing a little jig as she grabbed a bag of clothing from the back of Melody's car. "I am the oldest one here, but I plan on teaching you all how to have fun. The Lord's way, of course."

"Of course, Nonni. There is no other way." Melody followed her grandmother inside, lugging a big box of toys.

"It's always a good time when we do the work of the Lord and have fun in the Lord," Nonni assured her granddaughter as they put their load of toys and clothes on a nearby table. "You see, when we all work together, we have a good time. We are giving to others, spending time together, sharing our hearts. None of this sitting at home on the smartphone playing games."

"Hey, I like games." Doreena, Max's mother, gave her mother a hug. "But you're right, Momma, we have fun when we think of others."

"I raised a smart daughter." Nonni laughed and patted Doreena's cheek. "So, let's see what else Sierra would like for us to do."

Sierra looked at the piles of gifts, clothing and other items. "Okay, I have tables set up by age and gender. Let's start taking gifts to the appropriate tables. There is also a household item section and a table for parent gifts. We also need to start sizing and hanging the clothes on the lines we've strung at the back of the room."

"Let the fun begin," Kylie quipped.

They'd been working for a half hour, with Nonni leading them in some church songs, when Carson stepped into the room and announced that the food was ready. He scanned the crowd, saw his wife and couldn't hide the love he had for her. Sierra felt something she hadn't felt before. Envy. The emotion took her by surprise. She loved Kylie and had been so happy for her friend when Carson had returned to Hope and the two high school sweethearts reunited.

She'd never felt jealous of their relationship. Rather she'd been glad that it was them and not her stuck in the mire of those emotions.

Sierra had always known that a single moment, one event, could change a life. She'd experienced it in so many negative ways. Now, finding it happening in a positive way, it took her by surprise to look back and see how it had unfolded, how God had been at work.

A small child, a man willing to make a woman a cup of tea, and everything had changed. She thought about Bub and what that silly dog had also meant to her life. Because she found herself turning to him when the nightmares crashed in.

Looking around, she saw Nonni, Doreena, Melody and the other townswomen who were now a part of her circle. Max's family had shown her such love and acceptance. They'd shown her what a family could be.

"Are you going to come with us?" Kylie asked, a hand on Sierra's arm, drawing her back to the present.

"Of course I am. I was just thinking about this event and how God had His hand in orchestrating so much that has happened."

"Oh?" Kylie's eyes widened.

"Just go." Sierra gave her friend a little push toward her husband. "Carson is waiting for you."

"Yes, he is, isn't he?" Kylie got that look on her face. After being married for a couple of years, that look should have gone away, or so Sierra thought. But she'd been wrong before.

Sierra followed the crowd from the room and found that the men had set up tables in the kitchen and were serving hotdogs, brats, burgers and side dishes. There were several cooks, including Carson, Pastor Stevens, Isaac and Max.

"This was very nice of you all," Sierra said to Isaac as she went through the food line.

"It's the least we could do since you women are doing the rest of the work. We men don't mind doing the heavy lifting or the cooking." Isaac winked at his wife, who had stopped working to feed her daughter.

Rebecca glanced back over her shoulder at Sierra. "Do not believe him. This was all Jack's idea."

"I would have thought of it eventually," Isaac claimed.

"Of course you would have, honey." Rebecca shook her head. "No, he wouldn't have. He would have been at home watching football."

"The Chiefs might go to the Super Bowl." Isaac slid a burger on a bun and placed it on Sierra's plate. "Eat up, you need energy because Nonni informed us all that there's to be a dancing lesson after lunch."

"Oh, I don't dance," Sierra said.

"You do now," Max told her as she stopped at the table with side dishes. "And don't worry, we didn't make any of this. Holly did."

"Good thing, because none of us need food poisoning."

His hand went to his heart. "You wound me."

She laughed. "I doubt I've even made a dent in your self-confidence."

"I'll forgive you if you'll join me at table five."

"Are the tables numbered?"

He pointed to the table where his family sat together, hands joined in prayer. Her heart thumped at the sight of them. It was the kind of family that every child dreamed of when they didn't have that for themselves. Once, a long time ago, she'd prayed for a family that would sit at the table together, go to church together, cook dinner together.

"I don't know, I think Kylie…"

He arched a brow at her objection. "Scared?"

"No! Fine. Table five it is."

"I'll meet you there."

Sierra bypassed several groups of people who asked her to join them at their tables. It would have been easy to sit with Kylie and Carson at their table with the rest of the West clan. Or she could have sat with her friends from the ranch. Pastor Stevens and his wife, Tish, waved her toward their table. Everyone knew that she was the single among the many couples and families.

As everyone tried to draw her to their group, she realized she had people. A lot of people. Including this borrowed family that had welcomed her as one of their own.

Max. She didn't know if he was the sum total of the changes taking place or if he just happened to be where she was and her heart had included him. She couldn't compartmentalize things as she usually did. So she avoided. She sat next to Melody and pretended the conversation she really needed to have at the moment was about the Christmas event.

She ignored that Max had taken a seat across from her and was watching her, and that, for the first time, he looked as unsure as she felt.

Chapter Sixteen

The family sat around eating, joking and talking of Christmas. Max listened, sometimes chiming in, but mostly his eyes kept straying to the woman sitting across from him. Not once did she mention her Christmas plans, or seeing her family. He hadn't thought much about the fact that he took his family for granted. They'd always been there, always been close. Even when times were difficult, they'd had each other.

"You should join us for Christmas, Sierra." Nonni reached for Sierra's hand. "I know you have your celebration at the ranch, but perhaps you could have your time with them and with us. Tell her, Maximus, she should spend Christmas with us. We will go to the morning service at church and then home for lunch and gifts. In the evening, we will light candles and tell the story of the birth of Christ. It's a beautiful time to spend together. Be a part of our family this year, Sierra."

Sierra looked stricken. Max nearly reached for her hand, but he couldn't reach. Never mind the fact that his family would question their relationship. That would only put more pressure on her and make her more uncomfortable.

"I think it's up to Sierra, Nonni. They have traditions at the ranch just like we do at our house."

"Of course they do." Nonni looked at him as if he had just hatched. "I'm only saying she could spend time with us, too."

"I'll consider it," Sierra said.

"Good!" Nonni said as if it were decided. He knew his grandmother, and in her mind, there was no question about where Sierra would spend Christmas.

With them.

"Yes, good." Melody winked at him. "Nonni, how about that dance now?"

Nonni clapped her hands and beamed at Melody. "Thank you for reminding me. I want you to see how we will celebrate your wedding to Andrew. Organizing the reception is very important and much easier to show you now, with this big crowd to help."

Doreena put a hand over her mother's hand. "Momma, they might not all want to dance."

Nonni looked perplexed. "Who doesn't like to dance? Come on, let's get everything ready. Max, if you have the music on your phone, Sierra can put it on her musical system."

"Yes, I can do that if Max has the music."

"The music is very loud," Max warned.

"It isn't a problem. The sound system is at the front by the DJ booth," Sierra said and she didn't seem at all put off by his grandmother's suggestion.

"Got it."

Sierra winked at him and then she started to make her rounds, going from table to table, asking for participants. Max paused at the door, watching as she spoke to each group, smiling and gesturing with her hands to get her point across.

Suddenly a bomb hit him.

He didn't want to leave Hope.

He didn't want to leave her.

Just then, Nonni caught up with him as he headed for the DJ booth. She walked fast and talked fast, his grandmother. He thought she might have made an excellent salesperson. Or a lawyer. She had a gift of circling her conversation and then tightening it like a lasso.

"So, Grandson, since Andrew is not here, you and your Sierra will be the bride and groom. For demonstration only."

"My Sierra?" He felt heat climb his neck and he pulled on his shirt collar, which had suddenly grown tight.

"Oh, please, you're not so cool that we can't see what is happening. You light up when she is in the room."

"You make me sound like a teenage girl, Nonni."

"You're being purposely argumentative." She didn't look or sound pleased. "Trying to con an old woman is not right."

He took a deep breath and decided it was best to be agreeable to her plans. "What would you like us to do?"

"Hook up the music," she started, ticking off one finger. "And then everyone will act as if they're the family and wedding attendants. They will dance in with their scarves, everyone forms a circle, and then the bride and groom enter and join the circle. And then the dance."

"You'll have to show everyone the dance." He scrolled through his phone until he found the appropriate music. It was an Assyrian instrumental folk song.

"Of course I will show them. It would have been nice if Andrew could join us. But he's away with his family. I don't understand young couples today, living such separate existences." She arched a brow, as if asking him to give an explanation to the missing fiancé.

He knew better than to comment.

A few minutes later, Pastor Stevens was in charge of music and Max was standing outside the make-believe doors with Sierra. Carson and Kylie, Rebecca and Isaac were also a part of the pretend wedding party. Max looked at the group assembled. He could picture in his mind a wedding party that looked very similar to this one. And the bride looking up at him was the woman standing next to him right now.

"I really don't dance," she told him.

"It's very simple. It's more of a skip, really, and the bride has a scarf she dances with. The groom has a cane or something that is wrapped and tasseled. When we get to the circle, you take two crossover steps and then a few steps forward, and then, going back, you kick out with left leg, right leg, left leg and then sidestep again. Repeat."

"Got it." Her hand fluttered on his arm and then settled there. Everything around him grew fuzzy and he could only see her face.

Is this what it felt like, to stand with a woman, promising her forever? Did it feel this thick with emotion, this amazingly right? He leaned his face close to hers.

"You may now kiss the bride," Isaac teased, his loud voice piercing the strange bubble that had wrapped around Max in the past few moments.

Max jerked back, aware that he'd very nearly done something crazy.

The music started. They were instantly drawn into the charade his grandmother had created, with Melody calling out the names of couples and music playing in the background as people laughed and clapped. He and Sierra were announced last. They danced their way through the crowd and joined hands in the circle.

Nonni squeezed into the circle, taking Sierra's hand on one side and Kylie's on the other. Max's parents and Melody joined the circle on his side. The circle began to dance the steps clockwise. Sierra was laughing and breathless next to him.

When the song ended, they all collapsed into chairs.

"That was fun," Sierra whispered to him. "And kinda embarrassing at the beginning. What was that, Max?"

She meant the almost kiss.

He shook his head. "Let's take a walk." He stood up and took her hand. He didn't know what he meant to say but he knew that something had to be said.

Hopefully by the time he got her outside, his head would clear and he would be himself. In the next few minutes he needed the right words.

They assured everyone they would be right back. Sierra smiled and made excuses that she knew no one believed. Max led her out the front door and down a nearby trail to a water feature and gazebo. It was beautiful in the spring with flowers and green grass. In December the grass was brown and the roses had been clipped back for the season.

She let her mind wander, unsure because his hand still held hers, as if he didn't want to let go, and she wasn't sure she wanted him to let go. She didn't know anything about herself anymore because he'd changed everything.

They walked along the trail that surrounded the gazebo and his hand tightened on hers, as if he wasn't quite sure what he'd meant to do when he'd led her out here. She smiled, rather liking the idea of Max St. James being flustered.

"Where's your helicopter?" she joked as they made another loop on the path that normally would have been edged with flowers. She pulled him toward the bridge that led over the water feature and to the gazebo with its gingerbread trim and pretty benches.

"At the airport in a hangar." He let go of her hand and moved around the gazebo like a caged tiger. "Why do you ask?"

"Because I haven't seen it. Not that I've missed it. I most definitely have not missed it."

"I didn't think you had." He brushed a hand through his hair and leaned a hip against the ledge of the gazebo. "I could take you up in it sometime, if you want."

"You didn't bring me out here to talk about helicopters," she reminded him, taking a step closer to this man who had become such a big part of her life in less than three weeks.

Not just him, his family.

It frightened her, because keeping people on the edge of her life meant keeping them in a place where she felt safe.

"About the dance..." He brushed his hands over his face. "My grandmother did that on purpose."

"Oh, she must be in trouble, you called her 'grandmother.' Not Nonni."

He grinned at her. "She's up to her matchmaking tricks and obviously working overtime. But that moment, before we danced, that was just...wow."

It had felt like their lives had collided. That there'd been no air to breathe, no chance to get away from that one moment.

"It was wonderful," she admitted, simplifying all she'd been thinking.

"Sierra, I want to spend time with you. I want to do more than meet up when there's a family event, church event or catastrophe."

"I've kind of liked those moments."

"I want to take you to dinner. Somewhere other than Hope."

"But you're leaving," she reminded him. "So we will have a dinner out once in a while when you come back to town? Is that what you're proposing?"

He sat on the ledge. "No, that isn't what I'm proposing. I really don't know what I'm proposing, because I've been blindsided by you. I do know that I want to see you again."

"Oh. Check yes or no, will you be my girlfriend?" she teased.

He didn't laugh. Or smile. He wasn't joking. But she needed to say or to do something because her heart was racing, wanting something so badly and knowing that this couldn't be real. Things like this didn't happen to her. And if they did, they ended badly.

"Sierra, I don't know how to make this work or what to do next. I only know that I want to be around you more."

"But you're going back to Dallas, to the life you've made there. I'm still going to be here in Hope."

"We can work this out."

She shook her head. "There's one other problem."

"What's that?"

She wished she could sink into the floor of the gazebo. "I don't know what I'm feeling, and that isn't fair to you. Max, I love your family. I seriously want them to be my family. And you're amazing and wonderful. Everything a girl should want. But I'm afraid I'll do something stupid and muck things up between us. Or I'll figure out that it wasn't us, it was Christmas and having a family like yours to spend time with. What if that is all I'm feeling?"

His eyes widened and he laughed a little. "You're being serious?"

She nodded, wishing she wasn't about to cry. "I'm so serious. This is what I meant about making a mess of things. But I've never had a real family, not like yours. I love their meals, the honeymoon blanket, the dance."

"Can't you like us all? I mean, obviously like me a little more than you like them. But can't we be a package deal?"

"I don't like kissing them, I'm sure." It helped, to tease a little. But inside she was falling apart. "I don't want to drag you into my life just because I want your family."

She brushed at the tears rolling down her cheeks, even though she was laughing. Laughter was better than the pain of knowing this wouldn't end well.

"Sierra, I want to laugh with you more often. I want to hold you when you're afraid."

"This sounds like a proposal. I thought we were just discussing having dinner somewhere other than Holly's."

"That's what we are discussing," he agreed, sitting next to her on the bench. "I'm sure I said everything all wrong and now we have this gap between us and I really want to know that you might someday consider having dinner with me."

"I have to remind you that you're leaving, going back to Dallas. And in my experience, long-distance relationships rarely work out. I didn't expect to like you or your family so much. It scares me and I don't know what to do."

"It did happen quickly," he agreed. "And maybe I should have let the dust settle before I said something."

"Right. Like buying a car."

"I would never regret you."

"You might," she said. "You don't really know me. I'm like the shiny new thing that you think will make you happy but then you get it home and find out just how broken it is and there's no return policy. You're stuck with the broken thing."

"I hope that isn't how you see yourself, because it isn't how I see you. I see you as one of the strongest people I've ever met. But you don't know how amazing you are."

"I'm not amazing. I'm afraid. I'm sitting here wondering if I'm about to lose someone who was becoming a friend, all because I know I can't take the next step for fear I don't know myself well enough to let you in. I'm not sure I'm ready for more than friendship, and when I do let someone in, I want to be able to give them more."

He'd been standing on the opposite side of the gazebo but he moved to join her on the bench. She closed her eyes as he touched her cheek, then leaned to touch his lips to hers for a sweet kiss that felt like goodbye. When he broke it off, he looked deep into her eyes.

"Find yourself, Sierra. But know that I've already figured out who you are and I like the person I've gotten to know."

Then he walked away, leaving her shattered, wishing for something she couldn't quite grasp.

Her heart ached as she watched him go. She wanted to call him back but she knew, deep down in her heart, that wasn't enough. She didn't want pieces of him, she wanted all of him. And she wanted to give him all of her.

Chapter Seventeen

"Are you okay?" Kylie asked Sierra for about the dozenth time since they'd arrived at the Stable on Saturday evening, the night of the Christmas at the Ranch event.

Sierra gave the same answer she'd given every other time Kylie asked. "Of course I'm okay."

"Nope, you're not anything close to okay," Kylie responded. She reached down to pet Bub, who had been to the vet the previous day and had his cast taken off. He still limped a bit but he was happy to be back on his feet and back on duty.

Not that the broken leg had stopped him from doing his job. Since last Sunday he'd been sleeping in Sierra's bed, even though she'd had to lift him up and down each time.

Sierra went through the building, turning on lights. The chapel glowed with Christmas lights, a couple of dozen Christmas trees and the soft glow of the chandeliers. There would be music to start the evening and then a reading of the Christmas story. She loved that it would be here, in this chapel that had come to mean so much to her.

Kylie had followed her into the chapel and she put an

arm around Sierra's shoulders as she surveyed the work that had been done. "This is amazing."

"Thank you. It does look nice."

Kylie gave her a sharp and intuitive look. "You're one of my very best friends. You know that, right?"

"I know." Sierra smiled. "I feel the same way."

"So?"

Sierra sighed. "Is this the part where you want me to tell you what's bothering me?"

"Yes."

"Okay. Last Sunday, when we were setting this all up, Max and I had a moment."

Kylie got a look in her eyes but she didn't say anything.

"We talked and I told him I don't know what I feel for him, because I've never had a family and his family is so amazing and I love being around them. And what if I like the idea of his family more than I like him." She cringed now as she said it to her friend. "I'm such an idiot."

"Not an idiot, but wow." Kylie tried to stifle a giggle.

"That isn't nice." She wandered farther into the chapel, hoping to find some of the peace she seemed to have lost. "He lives in Dallas and I live here. He wanted to know if sometimes when he's here, if maybe we could go out to dinner. And I don't want to risk my heart that way."

"Makes perfect sense to me."

"Does it?" Sierra wasn't so sure.

"Yeah, it does."

Sierra looked around the chapel, finding it just as golden in the evening light as in the morning. "This is my place. I belong here, at this ranch, with all of you. I've never belonged anywhere. But now? Kylie, now I want to belong to someone. I don't want a casual date from time to time when he's in town. Not if it means he goes back to his world and I stay in mine." She bent down to

Bub to give him a kiss on his head. "I want to belong to a person. Maybe all of this happened so that I can realize that I'm okay and I can be loved. I can hug someone and not panic, kiss someone and not fear."

"That's possible," Kylie said in her understated way.

"But?"

"But I know that you don't give your emotions away without thinking through every single aspect of the relationship, and I know that you've been testing the waters with Max because you're drawn to him."

"I am, but I fear what might happen later on down the road. I feel like I'm finally healing, like I'm more whole than I've ever been in my life, but what if my brokenness hurts him?"

"It won't." Kylie raised a hand when she started to object. "And if it does? He's a grown man, he can handle it. He can handle your insecurities. If he loves you, he can handle it. Carson and I were both pretty broken people when he came back to Hope. We took two broken people and we made a whole."

"My parents were both broken people and they were never whole. They couldn't fix each other because they needed to work on themselves."

Kylie grimaced. "They were dysfunctional and they hurt each other and their child. I think the difference is that some of us lean on each other and become whole together. Some people keep each other broken and hurting."

Sierra did something she'd never done before. She grabbed Kylie and gave her a hug. "I'm so glad you're my friend."

She walked off, wiping at the tears that trickled down her cheeks. She wished she hadn't met Max St. James because meeting him meant missing him. Missing his family. That was the problem. She loved them all.

She loved him.

The arena area was brightly lit and decorated with Christmas trees. The gifts were spread out, each area cordoned off to keep them separate. The parents would get a card and go from one section to another, the cards signed after each section. It would keep things moving and less chaotic than people rushing from place to place.

Melody entered the room looking a little overwhelmed. Eyes wide, she came to stand by Sierra. "Are you okay?"

Sierra nodded. "Of course I am."

"I'm so glad you're a planner. I'm not. I can come up with an idea but I definitely couldn't have done this, not this efficiently with so little time."

"I love organizing, it makes me happy." She had never thought of it before, that need to organize, to make things neat.

"Really? Being organized makes me feel good but the act of getting organized is…" Melody shook her head.

"I think it must have happened in my childhood." Sierra said it quietly, not realizing she was speaking out loud.

"What?" Melody looked lost.

"The need to be organized. Making order out of chaos. It's what I did to comfort myself. My home life was a little chaotic and I would find solace in organizing. I would go to my room and organize my closets, dresser, whatever. And if my parents weren't at home, I organized the kitchen. And I baked."

"I'm sorry, I didn't know."

"No, I know. It isn't something I like to talk about." Sierra glanced at her watch. "I think we should be ready. People will be showing up soon."

"Oh, of course." Melody started to walk away but Sierra stopped her.

"I forgot to tell you, I'm going to buy the Cupcake Café!"

Melody's smile returned. "I'm so glad. You're perfect for that place. What about the Stable, though?"

"I'll continue to help manage it but I think Glory will take over. She's a romantic at heart and she'll plan beautiful weddings." Sierra made herself smile. "Ok, let's get this party started."

They were waiting at the doors when the first buses and cars started to arrive. Workers were in the kitchen getting the food prepared for a buffet-style meal. The music ministry from one of the local churches had set up in the chapel.

The first family through the doors was Patsy with her children. Linnie gave her a big hug as if she'd been missing her for days.

"Didn't I just see you a little over an hour ago?" Sierra asked Linnie.

"Yep," Linnie said. "But now it's Christmas."

"Well, not quite, but it's Christmas in this chapel."

Patsy reached for Sierra's hand and held it tightly. "I am so very glad that this chapel found Linnie and she found you."

"Me, too." Sierra couldn't believe how much had happened in the past few weeks. "It's been a journey."

Nearly two hundred people packed into the chapel. Some were there to support the service, others were there for their children.

Sierra stood at the back of the chapel listening to the choir voices raised in not so perfect harmony. When they began "Silent Night," her eyes went misty. She closed them and sang along, quietly.

She wished Max was here. But he wasn't. His mother had told her he'd flown back to Dallas. He had business to take care of there. She wished he could see what they'd accomplished. She wanted him to hear the music in this chapel, see the story of the Nativity read by Jack and let the laughter of children wash over him as they discovered Christmas gifts, cakes, cookies and other treats.

She had Nonni, Aldridge, Doreena and Melody. His family. She realized that, without him, it wasn't the same.

He hadn't said goodbye.

Max sat at his desk with the view of the Dallas skyline and he was miserable. A knock on the door stopped him from doing… Nothing.

"What's going on in here?" His business partner, Roger Anderson, walked through the door, leaning heavily on the cane he hated using. It was that injury that had brought the two of them together. Max had been developing software. Roger had wanted to develop something to keep soldiers safer in the field. A training program to teach them real-life exercises.

The two of them had gone to college together and now they were best friends and business partners.

"So?" Roger asked.

"Just thinking."

"Uh-oh, this can't be good. I haven't known you to think much about anything other than making money for the past eight years."

"Yeah, well, sometimes a guy gets a wake-up call."

"This has 'female' written all over it. You've met a woman."

Max tapped his pen on the desktop. "Yeah, I guess I have."

"And she rejected you!"

"You don't have to look so happy about that."

Roger sank heavily into the chair next to the desk.

"I'm not happy, I'm just glad to see you having some real human emotions. I was starting to worry."

"I have emotions."

"Maybe, but you've put everything on hold to be a businessman. You know, you can do both. You can have a business *and* a life. This business is built, Max. You have a partner who can do more. You have an assistant who is dynamite. Dude, why are you here?"

"Running the business," Max said.

"Yeah, right. You're safe here. You know what you're doing and you rarely fail. But at relationships, you kind of stink."

"Great. Thanks."

"I'm just being honest." Roger sat back in the chair, stretching his leg in front of him. "Have you been honest with this woman?"

"Yeah, I have."

"Bought her flowers?"

He cleared his throat. "I actually am going to buy her a horse."

"Really, a horse. Because every woman wants a horse."

"I think this one does."

"When am I going to meet her?"

Max shrugged and looked down at his vibrating phone. A call from his dad. He let it go to voice mail.

"I'm not sure," he answered Roger. "I have work to get done here. Being gone a month, things got behind."

"No, they didn't."

"You're saying I'm not needed here?" Max asked.

"Nope, I'm saying you did a good job from your Hope office."

"Of course."

Roger pushed to his feet. "I want you to know that you're needed in this office but you also need to follow your heart. The office is going to be here, you can fly in, check on things. You can run it remotely from that farm you insisted on buying. But a good woman won't wait for long. I'm just going to put this out there for you to think about. In a year, will it bother you to see her walking down the street with another man?"

"You're a great friend, Roger. But respectfully—go away!" Max said.

Roger made his way from the room. At the door, Max stopped him. "She isn't sure if she likes me or the idea of my family."

Roger turned around, resting his hand on the door for support. "Ouch, that couldn't have been good on the ego."

"It doesn't have anything to do with my ego. Could a woman fall for my family and I'm like the…"

"Icing on the cake?" Roger chuckled.

"Yeah."

"I mean, I guess that could happen." Roger took a step from the room. "I've met your family. I'm half in love with them myself. If Nonni was younger…"

Max wadded up a scrap piece of paper and tossed it at his friend. "Thanks for nothing."

"Always here to help."

Max went back to work. But his phone was buzzing with a voice mail from his dad. He listened, then he put away his files, locked his cabinet and left his office.

Chapter Eighteen

"Where are you going, Sierra?" Linnie followed Sierra to the front door of their apartment.

"I have to go get a few things for Christmas. Remember, it's tomorrow. We're going to have dinner with Jack and open presents in the morning."

Linnie hugged her waist. "I love you."

Patsy reached for her daughter's hand. "Are you sure you don't need help at the church?"

"Nope, I've got this," Sierra assured her. She hoped it was convincing. "I'm going to take some muffins over. They want a few treats for people to pick up with a cup of coffee before the service. You're going to meet me at Holly's in an hour, right?"

"If you're sure." Patsy seemed hesitant. That worried Sierra. She had one job to do. Surely she could convince Patsy to meet them at the diner.

"Of course we want you with us. We know it's last-minute but we want to get together this evening. And, of course, bring your mom." Sierra pushed on. "She'll love the café."

"Thank you, Sierra. I hope you know how much we love and appreciate you."

"Patsy, you and the kids mean a lot to us." She gave the other woman a quick hug. "I'll see you at the café. One hour. Oh, and will you stop and pick something up for me in town? I know this sounds crazy but I just remembered that I'm supposed to get cookies from a church member who lives on Sunset Drive. Do you know that street?"

"I think I do. It's off Lakeside, to the left."

"That's the one. The house is the last one on the left. They have a lot of Christmas lights."

"Just get them and bring them to the church?" Patsy asked.

"If you don't mind. I know that's a hassle, but it would help me out so much."

"I'll take care of it."

Sierra said a final goodbye and walked out, feeling very pleased with herself. She'd pulled it off. On her way to the car, she saw a trailer backed up to the barn. She slid the muffins in the back seat and again glanced in the direction of the barn. Everyone was supposed to be in their places. Isaac loading horses wasn't on the schedule.

She headed his way, ready to tell him that he was supposed to be in town. And then she saw the flash of gray as Isaac led a horse forward. The horse whinnied and fought against the lead rope. She ran the rest of the way to the barn.

"What are you doing?" she yelled as she ran.

"Loading Buckshot." Isaac turned the horse in a circle and took aim at the opening, leading the horse again.

"Why? Why are you loading him up? What are you doing?"

"We sold him." Isaac stepped the horse through the opening and closed the back. Buckshot whinnied, thrashing against the side of the trailer.

"No. You can't do this to him. This is his safe place. This is where he belongs, where he's loved."

"Sierra, calm down. You have to get yourself together. He's a horse. He has a new owner."

She pounded on him, crying. She felt herself losing the battle with Isaac and her emotions.

"You can't do this." She leaned against him and felt his hand on her back. "Isaac, don't."

Bub circled them, trying to figure out the situation. He growled low at Isaac and moved in behind Sierra.

"Call off your dog."

"I don't think I can. I'm so angry and hurt. I can't even talk to you. I have to go. I have somewhere I have to be, something I can't walk out on. But please, Isaac, please don't." She wiped away the tears that were falling.

Buckshot whinnied softly. She climbed up on the side of the trailer and brushed his velvety-soft nose. "I'll get you back. I promise."

"Sierra…"

"He's mine," she told Isaac.

"I know, just listen."

She kept walking, whistling softly for her dog to follow. She wasn't going to fall apart again. Tonight was about Patsy and her children. She was going to make it through this night, this week, this life.

Her heart desperately wanted Max. She'd never needed anyone, or so she'd always told herself. But tonight she wouldn't lie to herself.

She needed Max.

She needed to confide in him, lean on him, tell him she was lost without him.

Max had a plan, even if it seemed crazy. It had taken time. It had taken resources. Somehow, someway, it would work out.

He watched as Isaac backed the trailer up to the lot next to the feed store. The horse inside whinnied and stomped the trailer floor, raising a ruckus that could probably be heard all over town. Maybe this hadn't been such a great idea. It was starting to look downright dangerous.

Isaac jumped down from the truck and headed his way, looking meaner than a snake. That didn't make a lot of sense.

"I might never forgive you for this." Isaac glared as he opened the back of the trailer.

"What's wrong?"

"She caught me. I thought she was gone. I knew her car was there but I thought she was with Kylie."

Max groaned. "Sierra saw you loading this horse?"

"Yes, she did, and let me tell you, I'm holding you responsible for my bruises and her tears. Man, she's upset. I had no idea this horse meant that much to her. I'm surprised you noticed."

"Yeah, I noticed. I didn't want her to be upset. You should have just told her."

"You told me to keep it a secret, so I did." Isaac stomped around, still fuming.

"Okay, well, hopefully she'll forgive us."

"Yeah, well, maybe she will and maybe she won't. But I've never seen her that upset."

They led the horse from the trailer and hitched him to the small buggy they'd been training him to pull. "So you're sure he's safe."

"He's safe. I couldn't believe it myself. I think he's definitely pulled a wagon or a cart, something." Isaac settled the harness and they backed Buckshot to the cart with its solar-powered Christmas lights.

Isaac glanced back at Max. "The one who isn't safe is you. Sierra is going to hurt you."

"Yeah, well, I hope that's not the case. I hope that, after we talk, she's going to see that we can have a future together."

Isaac slapped him on the back. "You know, I kind of hope so, too. First I want her to give you the same thrashing she gave me. But I do hope that in the end she gives you a chance."

"Thanks, I think."

"I mean it, Max. I want the best for both of you."

They finished harnessing the horse and Max was surprised by how calm the animal was. He climbed into the buggy and took a seat on the narrow bench, gathering up the reins.

"You've got this?" Isaac asked as he stepped away.

"I've got this. We practiced earlier today. I'm going to drive the buggy up and, just a few houses down, Matt will watch it for me. Text me when you get there and let me know if Sierra is there."

"Will do. See you there."

After Isaac walked away, leaving his truck and trailer parked, Max sat on the bench seat thinking about Sierra and this plan of his. He'd prayed about it, often. He'd prayed for her, to be happy, to be whole. He had considered that maybe that was his purpose in her life, to pray for her. And then he'd prayed for guidance. So here he was, sitting in a wagon behind the gray horse she loved.

The horse shifted from hoof to hoof and the harness rattled a bit.

Max understood the animal's impatience. He had never been this impatient in his life. He had never missed anyone this much. He had prayed about this moment, prayed for her and for himself. His phone buzzed and he glanced down at the text from Isaac with a kissing emoji at the end. He chuckled as he gave the reins a little flick and Buckshot took off at a sedate walk.

The air was cold and damp as he rolled up Lakeside Drive. It was Christmas Eve, all the stores were closed but Christmas lights decorated the tiny town of Hope. The tree at the end of the street was strung with lights and decorated with large red and silver ornaments. In the distance he could hear piped Christmas music playing from a hidden speaker.

Ahead he could see the cars streaming onto Sunset Drive. He waited until the traffic slowed and cars were parked, then he gave Buckshot the cue to move forward. The horse picked his way down the road, his hooves beating out a steady rhythm.

Max didn't want to take anything away from Patsy's moment so he drove the horse to the driveway of one of her neighbors and hopped down from the seat.

"Nice-looking horse, Mr. St. James."

"Thank you, Matt. You sure you don't mind holding him for a few minutes?"

"I don't mind at all. I hope someday you'll let me take my girl for a ride using this buggy."

"You've got it."

He left the teenager and the horse and walked up the sidewalk to the house that had been renovated for Patsy and her children. Patsy wasn't due to arrive for another fifteen minutes.

He entered the house through the back door and saw Sierra standing with friends from church and the ranch. His parents were there, too. Max circled around, finding a way to get near Sierra.

When he walked up behind her, she stiffened and then turned around, as if she'd known it was him. Her eyes were rimmed with red. She'd been crying over the horse. He wanted so badly to take her in his arms.

"Max," she whispered. "I didn't know you were going to be here."

"I couldn't miss this," he explained.

"No, of course not." She took a breath. I'm sure your family is glad to have you home for Christmas."

"They are. They think that if I'm home, it means you'll be joining us for Christmas dinner. I told them that would be up to you."

"Here she comes," someone called out from the front of the house. The lights were off except for the Christmas lights inside and out. The house smelled of new paint, new carpet and lemon-scented cleaners.

From outside he could hear car doors slamming, then children talking and laughing. As Patsy approached the porch, a light came on and the door opened. Kylie and several others greeted Patsy and told her to come inside. Others yelled, "Surprise!"

The living room light came on, illuminating a living space furnished, decorated and ready for a new family. The tree in the corner twinkled with lights, and presents were wrapped and ready for Christmas morning. Patsy looked around the crowded room and started to cry.

Next to him, Sierra sobbed.

He pulled a tissue from his pocket and handed it to her. "Good thing I planned ahead."

She took it and wiped her eyes. Then she moved closer to him and he put his arm around her.

Patsy drew her children close. "I'm not sure what's going on."

"Patsy, we hope you will be very happy in this new house." Jack West, with his housekeeper Maria's help, approached Patsy, holding out a set of keys. "A lot of work went into this old house but we hope it will be a home you and the children enjoy for years to come."

"I don't know what to say. I can't pay for this."

Jack patted her back. "I think we'll figure something out."

"Can we sleep here?" Linnie asked.

Kylie moved in, taking her by the hand. "Let me give you a tour of your new home, Linnie. And it even has a fenced-in backyard. It also has dressers filled with clothes and there are sheets and blankets on the beds. Unless you want to be at the ranch tomorrow morning, you can definitely stay here tonight."

"Linnie, we're home." Patsy hugged her daughter. The little girl broke loose to wrap her arms around Sierra.

"Goodbye, Sierra."

"I'll see you tomorrow, Linnie."

The room remained crowded with those still wanting to give Patsy their well-wishes.

Max took Sierra by the hand and led her out the front door. "Do you mind if we talk?" he asked.

She shook her head. "I don't mind."

He led her down the sidewalk. As they walked, snow began to fall.

He'd planned this moment for days. Each scenario had been different, some ended with him alone, others ended with her telling him how much she'd missed him.

As long as she was here by his side, he felt as if he had a fighting chance.

The snow had begun to fall as they walked away from Patsy's house. It was the perfect snow, with big flakes that fell softly to the ground, blanketing everything in whiteness. The perfect Christmas snow. Everything was strangely silent but in the distance she heard a bell and the jangle of a harness. It couldn't be a sleigh, not with this slight amount of snow, but someone was definitely out for a carriage ride.

She envied them. But thinking of a carriage ride made her think of Buckshot and how sad and confused he must be. The ranch had been his home for several years. He'd been loved at the ranch. He'd felt safe there.

She and Buckshot were very much alike. And just as they'd started to feel safe, someone upended their lives. She wiped at the tears that started to fall again.

"Sierra, are you okay?"

She sighed. "I'm fine. Isaac sold my horse."

"Oh."

That was it? He wasn't going to offer words of comfort? She really needed to be comforted. "Max, why are you here?"

"To give you this," he said in a mysterious voice. Then she realized he'd led her straight to the horse and buggy. A gray horse.

"Buckshot?"

The horse whinnied a little and jerked away from the boy who had been holding him. The horse dribbled the apple he'd been chomping and shook his head, clearing the snow that had settled on his steel-gray coat.

"How did you get my horse?" Sierra asked the teenager.

Max put an arm around her. "I left Buckshot with him."

"You have my horse?" She looked from Max to the horse and buggy. "You have him harnessed to a buggy?"

"Yes, I do. I have your horse harnessed to a buggy." He handed Matt another twenty bucks and took the reins from him. "Sierra, will you go for a drive with me?"

"Go for a drive?"

He took her hand and led her forward. "Please."

She looked up at him, the snow swirling around them, catching the light from nearby streetlamps. Most of his face was shadowed by his cowboy hat, but she saw his dark eyes, saw a depth of emotion that took her by surprise.

"Please," he repeated.

She nodded and he helped her into the buggy.

"There's hot cocoa in thermal mugs in the basket," he told her. "There's also a blanket to cover your legs. The snow is extra, even I couldn't plan that."

"That's God's handiwork," she told him as she opened the basket and pulled out the mugs of cocoa.

Max led the buggy through the yard and then went at a gentle trot down the road. Buckshot didn't seem to like to be ridden but he acted as if he enjoyed pulling the buggy.

"You took my horse." There was an accusation in Sierra's tone.

"I bought him," Max corrected. And, after a pause, he added, "For you. He's your horse now and no one will take him from you."

"I was so afraid he'd been sold to strangers. And the whole time I was thinking I needed you here with me." She sipped on hot cocoa as tears fell. "You shouldn't make a girl cry, not if you intend to say nice things to her."

"I'm sorry for making you cry, but my intentions were to make you happy. That's what I want to do, Sierra. Every single day, I want to make you happy. I want you to know that you can love my family as long as you love me, too."

"I do love you, silly man." She kissed his cheek. "I love you so much and I've been miserable without you."

"About that... I've been pretty miserable myself. I realized I can actually commute to Dallas when necessary but operate my business from Hope. A funny thing happened to me in the past week. This business has been my life for several years, but now I want something more. I want a life with you."

Snow continued to fall as Max finally brought the buggy to a stop near the church. Snow covered the ground and decorated the evergreens that stood next to the church. The snowflakes sparkled in the lights as they drifted slowly to the ground.

"Sierra, I love you. I know that this happened faster than either of us ever imagined. I know that we need more time to get to know each other. I also know that I want that time with you."

"I want that, as well. I don't want you to go away again, not unless I'm going with you."

"Do you trust me?"

She put a hand to the warm skin of his cheek. "I trust you with my heart, with my future."

He captured her mouth in a hot cocoa kiss as snowflakes covered their hair, their jackets, their faces.

Sierra was home. In this town, in his arms, she was home. She'd never considered what it would feel like to find a place and a person that she wanted forever. Now she knew. It felt like the world had righted itself and Max was there, holding her steady.

Slowly he kissed her. When he pulled away, Sierra looked up at the night sky and said a silent thank-you.

Epilogue

Thirteen wasn't supposed to be a lucky number. Max didn't believe in luck. He wasn't superstitious. He had a faith in God, for his life, his future and for this day. Thirteen months ago, he'd helped find a little girl who had gone missing. And he'd found Sierra.

She'd been almost as lost as the child that they'd both wandered upon that day.

That day had changed so many lives. It had changed his life. It had changed Sierra's life.

Thirteen was just a number, but today it meant everything to him.

Thirteen was the number of roses in Sierra's bridal bouquet. Red and white roses in a bouquet of freesia and wildflowers. Because he always thought of Sierra when he smelled wildflowers.

Next to him, Isaac laughed a little. "You going to make it through this, St. James?" Isaac asked.

"I'll be just fine." He stood a little taller with his groomsmen at his side. Isaac and Carson West. His business partner, Roger.

The bridesmaids stood silently, not joking, not teasing. They were waiting for the bride. As was he. He couldn't

wait to repeat the wedding dance they'd learned last year.
Nonni had made them practice just two days ago and
she'd smiled as she'd paired up the guests. Roger might
think he was happily single, but Max was certain Nonni
had plans for him.

Suddenly the "Wedding March" began and the bride
stepped forward, her hand on Max's dad's arm. She had
invited her mother to the wedding, not her father. She
was working on forgiving but she still struggled with
the pain her father had caused.

But today, none of that mattered. Today she became
his bride. His forever.

Aldridge St. James patted Sierra's hand that rested on
his arm. She was glad he had hold of her because she was
so happy she felt she might float away. Today she would
get married in the chapel that had changed her life, to
the man who had changed her life.

One Christmas after they'd met, they were now becoming man and wife. She'd insisted on waiting until
Christmas because they'd had a beautiful Christmas proposal and now they would have the beautiful Christmas
wedding.

"Are you ready for this?" Aldridge asked.

"Yes. Is it crowded?" she asked as he led her to the
entry of the chapel.

"It is. You have so many people who love you, Sierra."

"I have so many people that I love," she told him. "Including all of you."

"We're so thankful our son found you. You're the
woman we prayed for, the one he was waiting for."

The music started. The door opened and he led her up
the aisle toward her groom, who waited at the front of the
chapel. He stood straight in his neatly tailored suit. Isaac,

Carson and Max's business partner, Roger, stood behind him. On the other side, Kylie, Eve and Patsy waited, holding their bridesmaid bouquets.

Kylie's son Adam was the ring bearer. He appeared to be studying one of the flower arrangements. The flower girls, Maggie and Linnie, were peeling petals off roses. Sierra laughed a little at the sight because it wasn't perfect but it was perfect for her.

As she got closer to the altar, she saw Pastor Stevens wink. She knew the reason. Because he'd told them more than once not to sweat the wedding. Mistakes would happen. Things would go wrong. In the end, he'd told them, remember that it isn't the wedding that defines your life, it's the marriage. The wedding is a few hours and a lot of money. The marriage is forever.

Her gaze connected with Max's. One year ago, she'd been afraid of giving her heart. Of losing her heart. She'd had so many fears.

Today she felt fearless.

Today she would become Sierra St. James, a wife.

She was also a survivor.

* * * * *

*If you loved this story,
pick up the other books
in the Mercy Ranch series,*

Reunited with the Rancher
The Rancher's Christmas Match
Her Oklahoma Rancher
"His Christmas Family"
in Western Christmas Wishes

*from bestselling author
Brenda Minton.*

Available now from Love Inspired!

Find more great reads at www.LoveInspired.com

Dear Reader,

Sierra Lawson has been a favorite character of mine from the conception of the Mercy Ranch series. I loved her dry sense of humor, her angst, her heart that she kept safely hidden. While writing the previous books, it only made sense to make the less-than-romantic veteran a wedding planner.

As she continued to evolve, I knew she needed a hero to show her that she is both strong *and* that she can trust and find love. The perfect hero came along unexpectedly in Max St. James. Gradually love came to Mercy Ranch's wedding planner. In the end she trusts that this man is hers, forever.

Thanks for reading *The Rancher's Holiday Hope*. For more information on me and the Mercy Ranch series, find me on Facebook at Brenda Minton Author, or on Twitter at @brendaminton.

Happy Holidays!
Brenda

WE HOPE YOU ENJOYED THIS BOOK!

New beginnings. Happy endings.
Discover uplifting inspirational
romance.

Look for six new Love Inspired
books available every month,
wherever books are sold!

LoveInspired.com

COMING NEXT MONTH FROM
Love Inspired®

Available December 17, 2019

FINDING HER AMISH LOVE
Women of Lancaster County • by Rebecca Kertz
Seeking refuge from her abusive foster father at an Amish farm,
Emma Beiler can't tell anyone that she's former Amish whose family was
shunned. She's convinced they'd never let her stay. But as love blossoms
between her and bachelor Daniel Lapp, can it survive their differences—
and her secrets?

THE AMISH MARRIAGE BARGAIN
by Marie E. Bast
May Bender dreamed of marrying Thad Hochstedler—until he jilted her for
her sister with no explanation. Now, with Thad widowed and a single father,
the bishop insists they conveniently wed for the baby girl. When May learns
the real reason for his first marriage, can they rediscover their love?

A HOPEFUL HARVEST
Golden Grove • by Ruth Logan Herne
On the brink of losing her apple orchard after a storm, single mom
Libby Creighton can't handle the harvest alone. Reclusive Jax McClaren
might be just what her orchard—and her heart—needs. But he's hiding a
painful secret past...and love is something he's not quite sure he can risk.

HER SECRET ALASKAN FAMILY
Home to Owl Creek • by Belle Calhoune
When Sage Duncan discovers she was kidnapped as a baby, she heads to
a small Alaskan town to learn about her birth family—without disclosing her
identity. But as she falls for Sheriff Hank Crawford, revealing the truth could
tear them apart...

SNOWBOUND WITH THE COWBOY
Rocky Mountain Ranch • by Roxanne Rustand
Returning home to open a veterinary clinic, the last person Sara Branson
expects to find in town is Tate Langford—the man she once loved. Tate is
home temporarily, and his family and hers don't get along. So why can't
she stop wishing their reunion could turn permanent?

A RANCHER TO TRUST
by Laurel Blount
Rebel turned rancher Dan Whitlock is determined to prove he's a changed
man to the wife he abandoned as a teen...but Bailey Quinn is just as set
on finally ending their marriage. When tragedy lands Dan as the guardian
of little orphaned twins, can he give Bailey all the love—and family—she's
ever wanted?

———————————

LICNM1219

SPECIAL EXCERPT FROM

*Can a mysterious Amish child bring two wounded
souls together in Cedar Grove, Kansas?*

Read on for a sneak preview of
The Hope *by Patricia Davids*
available December 2019 from HQN Books!

"You won't have to stay on our account, and we can look
after Ernest's place, too. I can hire a man to help me.
Someone I know I can…" Ruth's words trailed away.

Trust? Depend on? Was that what Ruth was going
to say? She didn't want him around. She couldn't have
made it any clearer. Maybe it had been a mistake to think
he could patch things up between them, but he wasn't
willing to give up after only one day. Ruth was nothing if
not stubborn, but he could be stubborn, too.

Owen leaned back and chuckled.

"What's so funny?"

"I'm here until Ernest returns, Ruth. You can't get rid
of me with a few well-placed insults."

She huffed and turned her back to him. "I didn't insult
you."

"Ah, but you wanted to. I'd like to talk about my plans
in the morning."

Ruth nodded. "You know my feelings, but I agree we
both need to sleep on it."

Owen picked up his coat and hat, and left for his uncle's farm. The wind was blowing harder and the snow was piling up in growing drifts. It wasn't a fit night out for man nor beast. As if to prove his point, he found Meeka, Ernest's big guard dog, lying across the corner of the porch out of the wind. Instead of coming out to greet him, she whined repeatedly.

He opened the door of the house. "Come in for a bit." She didn't get up. Something was wrong. Was she hurt? He walked toward her. She sat up and growled low in her throat. She had never done that to him before. "Are you sick, girl?"

She looked back at something in the corner and whined softly. Over the wind he heard what sounded like a sobbing child. "What have you got there, Meeka? Let me see."

He came closer. There was a child in an Amish bonnet and bulky winter coat trying to bury herself beneath Meeka's thick fur. Where had she come from? Why was she here? He looked around. Where were her parents?

Don't miss
The Hope *by Patricia Davids,*
available now wherever
HQN™ books and ebooks are sold.

HQNBooks.com

Get 4 FREE REWARDS!

We'll send you 2 FREE Books plus 2 FREE Mystery Gifts.

Love Inspired® books feature contemporary inspirational romances with Christian characters facing the challenges of life and love.

FREE Value Over $20

Discover wholesome and uplifting stories of faith, forgiveness and hope.

Join our social communities to connect with other readers who share your love!

Sign up for the Love Inspired newsletter at **LoveInspired.com** to be the first to find out about upcoming titles, special promotions and exclusive content.

CONNECT WITH US AT:

Facebook.com/groups/HarlequinConnection

 Facebook.com/LoveInspiredBooks

 Twitter.com/LoveInspiredBks

LISOCIAL2019